Virgin Call Girl

An Erotic Tale

A Wife Turns Her Husband Into a Call Girl!

By Barbara Deloto and Thomas Newgen

D1714031

Other books written by Barb and Tom
Shapeshifter
Changes
Changes II
Virgin Bride
Hypnotized

Table of Contents

Saturday Night Playtime

It was Saturday night and my wife Jenna and I had cleaned the house and gotten all our tasks done that day. We were going to do our usual Saturday night thing. I always got excited thinking about it. She'd usually have a new mini dress or some kind of sexy outfit she'd bought online, or at a store if she had time, for our special evening.

Jenna and I had showered and dressed for dinner. She was in a black, sheer overlay, mini dress with a deep V-neck. It fit her five foot one, one hundred and five pound body beautifully, hugging her curves, then flaring out following the angle of her hips. It floated around her thighs as she walked in her strappy Italian leather five-inch heel shoes. Her breasts swayed slightly in her thirty-two C push up bra with her walk from the dining room table to the kitchen. Her short, jet black, gelled hair, stayed firmly in place in the layers she emphasized with the gel.

I smelled Jenna's fragrance now as she brushed against me while we loaded the dishwasher. I had seen her spray that fragrance over her body as she stood in her garter belt and stockings before she slid into the dress. I looked into her bright blue eyes with the perfect black ring around the iris and the dramatic eyeliner and shadow as she leaned down to put the wine glasses into the machine. I couldn't resist putting my hand on her bottom and feeling it's firm yet fleshy feel.

She purred at me. "Mmm, I AM SOO horny tonight!" She turned and wrapped her arms around me looking down slightly at me. "Jessie, I'm a little taller than you are in these five inch heels and it feels good." She kissed me deeply on the lips running one of her long fingernailed hands through my hair below the ponytail. Then she pulled it while the other hand rubbed the front of my black silk dress pants.

Jenna leaned back pushing against my crotch with her thigh and looked into my eyes. "Ready for a drink? You look very handsome tonight in all black like that. With that blond hair in the ponytail with the waves on your back it's uh, mmm. Those silver blue eyes. Mmm, and I love the feel of the silk pants and shirt."

"Yea, they do feel nice. Probably cost as much to dry-clean them as they cost to buy though. Yea, I think I'll have a gin and tonic. You?"

"Don't be worrying about what it costs. We make plenty! Gin and tonic sounds good."

She released me and I turned to get the gin out and mix the drinks. "You're the one making more than three times what I make so it feels like you're the one paying for them. I guess it's just another of my insecurities."

She put her hands around my waist as I poured the gin into the tall crystal glasses over the ice. "Honey, you make great money as our number one programmer! So what if I make more. You wouldn't want to do what I do anyway."

"I know, it just feels weird having you be so far up the ladder at work and me being where I am."

"It's just our natures that's all. It's easy for me to be aggressive and determined whereas for you it's about creativity and logic, a strange blend but one that makes you the best at what you do. I couldn't do what you do and not many others could. It just doesn't pay as well as being a bitch does. Ha ha ha." She took her drink from my hand and turned to go into the great room. I followed her watching the dance her round, apple bottom did shifting back and forth beneath the fabric of the sheer dress as she walked in minced steps in those super high heels. My God she was gorgeous. How did I ever deserve her?

Jenna sat on the black leather love seat, adjusting her dress on her thigh to cover the top on her sheer black stockings. She patted the seat for me to join her as she bounced the foot of her crossed leg. "Sit down baby and stop worrying. We're so lucky to have jobs at the company we're at with the 30 hour work weeks, no dress code, progressive policies on earning extra time off when we work later and on and on."

"Yea, policies you drove into place. I know, it's good but I always feel so, uh, so insignificant sometimes. You always get whatever you set after no matter how difficult it may be. A truly powerful woman."

Jenna slugged down half of her drink and then opened her purse taking out a blue pill. She cracked it in half with her long pink fingernailed fingers and put the other half back into her purse. She handed me the one half. "Take this baby and let's not fuss about things. I want to see you come hard tonight."

I took the E.D. pill, not because I needed it but because it felt so good, and it made me as big as I could get. I got excited thinking about how I'd be feeling in a little bit. I felt myself throb in my slick, nylon missile thong Jenna bought me. The fabric of the thong slipped against the smooth silk of the pants. Jenna ran her hand over my crotch. "Mmm, see, this is going to be nice."

Jenna kissed me on the lips with her painted, pouty mouth and sucked my tongue. She pulled back from me and opened her purse once more to light a cigarette and drink her drink. She woke the laptop up with the remote and turned on the television selecting the auxiliary feed from the computer. "I found some new porn baby. I think you'll like it. The guys are all shaved smooth and hung like donkeys and the girls are tiny and built." Jenna put her lipstick stained smoke in the ashtray, which gave me another throb. For some reason, seeing lipstick on the filter of a cigarette was erotic to me.

"Built as good as you? Haven't seen one of them yet"

"Thanks sweetie! Na, not as good as me I guess, but the cocks are incredible!"

3

"Yea, huge four inchers, an inch and a half across, like mine right?"

"Oh silly, you have a cute cock. I love it. It's so smooth and silky. Now don't take this wrong but it doesn't look mean and tough like most guys with thick throbbing veins and a big purple helmet. It's nice and cute and pretty."

"Yea pretty, thanks for being nice baby." I ran my hand over her stockinged leg and wondered how long I could last if I put my monster inside of her tight wetness. I might last maybe a second or two? I felt myself get rock hard now, the blue pill doing its job.

The digital media loaded and started up. The guys on the previews looked like the guys Jenna worked out with at the gym. Built like rocks with big mean looking cocks. It made me hot as I thought about how hot Jenna will get tonight watching the videos and how hard she'll come imagining the toy inside her was the guy on the video.

"Could you get me the bag of toys and another drink sweetie? And could you put on your short black robe and take the pants and shirt off? I want to see that gorgeous shaved body of yours and I want to be able to see you come for me."

"Okay baby." I went and refilled our drinks, brought them back and put them on the tables. I went upstairs, changed into my robe and left on only my missile thong and put on the black satin robe. I grabbed the bag of Jenna's toys from the closet and brought them down stairs.

Jenna was now watching the video intently. She rubbed herself through the front of her dress, her hand between her legs. She sipped her drink using the other hand. She looked at me as I entered. "Thanks Jessie, you are a sweetie." She took the bag from my hand and took out a bullet vibrator and placed it on her clit through the dress. She purred like the vibrator now did. "Mmm. Gorgeous fucking cock isn't it?" She looked at the TV again as the 'gorgeous fucking cock' spread the woman's wetness and forced its way in slowly as the female porn star rolled her eyes back in her head as she felt the cock go in.

"Imagine feeling that Jenna. How good that must feel huh?"

"Oh yea baby. Hand me the middle size cock."

I handed her the flesh-like cock and balls that were about twice my size in length and girth and watched as Jenna lifted her dress hem and slipped it into her. Her now exposed garter belt, stockings and crotchless panties framed her wetness as the cock parted her and stretched her open.

"Better get me a towel Jessie. I'm so wet!"

I grabbed a towel from the bathroom, slipped it under her then sat beside her. My cock was throbbing in the air already and leaking precum. I drank my drink and watched the movie as the gorgeous hunk fucked the little hot babe's brain out. Jenna kept her penetrations in time with his cock entering and pounding the woman in the video.

Jenna came at the same time the woman in the movie did and then kept coming until the guy in the film shot his load inside of her. They showed it coming out around his cock as he grunted in his deep deep voice pulling the woman's hair as he did. Jenna came hard and yelled out, "Fuck yea! Like that! Fuck me! Ungh!" She came on the dildo stuffed deep inside of her as she pulled my head to her breast and had me pull down the fabric. I sucked her nipple, her body spasmed and clenched. I came uncontrollably and excessively on my thigh as she came, letting out a quiet moan as I did, giving myself away.

"You came already? Aww Jessie, I wanted to see it. Oh well, you'll come again. Now lick up all that come. We don't want to waste any since it will keep you horny with all the testosterone in it."

I flopped back on the couch spent from the orgasm and took a few deep breaths. I wiped the come off my thigh with my finger and ate it. "I wouldn't come so fast the first time if you'd let me jerk off without you. Whenever you have your period, you won't let me come and then, when you do, I can't help it. But, yea, I'll come again. No problem. You are so hot Jeanna. I love you."

"I love you too Jessie but you know I don't like when you come without me. It seems so, so, I don't know." Jenna said as she adjusted herself on the couch, the dildo still inside her with her legs crossed and one high heel bouncing across her other leg. She sipped her drink and lit a cigarette puffing on it as she continued bouncing her leg squeezing her thighs against the cock inside of her.

I felt myself start to harden again as I sipped my drink and watched Jenna. I rubbed myself against her stockinged thigh sliding my nylon-encapsulated dick against her.

"Ah, nice, I feel that. You got hard quick baby. Now don't come until I can watch okay?"

I pulled away and I took off the missile thong. I put it on the floor then I stroked myself with two fingers and a thumb watching Jenna.

She fast-forwarded to where the new guy, equally built and hung as the first, is pushing the girls legs behind her ears and pounding her hard and fast. Jenna got in time with her dildo and then turned to me. "Can you get me the big one baby? I'm ready for it."

I handed her the big ten inch one that was about two and a half inches across. The big balls at the bottom felt like real balls as they slipped in the sacks, the flesh felt firm, hard and silky. I took the other one from her and went to wash it off then I put it back into the bag ready for next time. Jenna always liked me to have all her toys ready to go at a moment's notice.

I knelt next to Jenna facing her on the couch. I watched as she spread her legs and forced that hunk of meat into her as she watched the video. She got in time again and she started coming over and over again.

Jenna ran out of steam after from what I could tell was about three long comes. She shut off the television and turned to me smiling.

"That was incredible baby. I take it that it was good for you too? You came real nice that first time even if it was too fast. Think you might have another one in there?"

"Uh, maybe in a little bit. You?"

"I'm not so sure. I'm kinda blissful feeling. But I wouldn't mind helping you come again. How about we have a drink and a smoke and then

I suck your cock." She smiled wickedly knowing it wouldn't take me long to come with that."

Jenna stood and adjusted her dress and stockings. She pulled her garter straps tight, and pushed her boobs into the dress adjusting her cleavage. She got us each another drink and we had a couple of smokes watching the weather channel. The weather lady was wearing some super high heels tonight and she looked pretty hot.

"I'll bet she's at her horny time of the month now. She's dressing hot tonight," Jenna said laughingly.

"Yea, hot like you are all the time Jenna!"

Jenna came back with the drinks and we sipped and watched the weather lady walk back and forth on the screen. Jenna slid her stockinged leg over mine and stroked my cock with two of her fingers and a thumb. She ran the thumb over the tip and made me shudder.

I grew to full size and Jenna dropped to her knees in front of me and took me in her mouth. She flicked the tip with her tongue and then ran it around the shaft as she looked up at me with her made up eyes. Her lipstick left a ring around the very base of my cock and she bobbed her head up and down.

She felt me tense up and I grabbed her head holding her tight while I thrust into her hot wet mouth as I came. I shot her mouth full as she caught it all. When I finished she hurried up and kissed me with it in her mouth passing it all to me to swallow.

"Mmm, I love sucking cock baby. I love giving you the come too since I know how it has all that testosterone in it and will help to keep you horny for me."

"Mmm." I drank the rest of my drink and put my head back on the couch. I fell asleep.

Friendly Advice

"Jessie really is the most wonderful husband," I thought to myself as I drove to the gym. Jessie had made us breakfast and I was out to my usual Sunday workout while he did things at home. My usual Sunday watching the hunks work out while I ran on the treadmills, did the stair climber and did some weights. While I was running, Cole ran along side of me as we normally did and we talked.

"How was your Saturday night Jessie? Did you satisfy yourself as usual? You always have that look on Sundays here."

"Of course, we had a great night! We always do! Why do you keep bugging me about that?"

"Because I know a guy that is five foot four doesn't usually have much to offer a gal. You know, guys like that really like to watch their wives more than they like to do them. Sometimes their called cuckolds and some of them really dress up nice like women."

"Oh Cole! Cut it out. What in the world is a cuckold!?"

I looked at my heart monitor and it had risen up from the thought of having Jessie watch a hunk and me.

"A cuckold is a guy that feels insignificant as a sexual partner and would rather see his wife pleased by someone that can make her crazy. He may not be small and he may not be insignificant either but he loves seeing his wife pleased.

"Sometimes, they really get off on dressing as women too, then they can partake in the guy as well without feeling gay. Then it's like they're two girlfriends and not husband and wife. They act like a woman and feel like a woman and then it doesn't feel bad to watch their wives or, even suck a cock. Or even have a guy fuck them in the bottom. Not all the guys are as lucky as your husband to have a body that would dress up well either. Some look like truckers in a skirt. Jessie would look incredible. I'm amazed someone as educated as you wouldn't be aware of those things. A doctorate in psychiatry?"

My heart monitor was increasing some more. I slowed down my running pace some and looked at Cole. His white teeth flashed. I looked over his body seeing his maleness push against his shorts with each jog he took. "So these cockolds__"

"CUCKolds." He flashed his white teeth at me with a big grin.

"So, cuck-olds, not cock olds. Yea, psychiatry but my emphasis was not on sexual issues by the way. Okay, so these, cuckolds, these guys actually enjoy watching their wives and some of them actually like dressing up because you say it takes away the guilt? Doesn't matter if they have a body to dress as a woman well or not but some of them like to just look and feel like women anyway. So then, it feels to them like it's two girls together. If they're crossdressed then they don't feel like it's the husband watching the wife. And some just like to watch and not dress like women. They can be big or small and some like to dress just to dress and don't care if they watch their wives but you think Jessie will do both huh?"

"Yea, that's it. Good job doctor."

"Well, Jessie is too manly to do that. Either of them! Never mind both."

"Ha ha ha, manly yea right."

"Not physically maybe but mentally."

"Trust me, he can be converted. Just get him to like silky things first. Don't let him come without them. Introduce more and more women's things. Have him shave his body."

"He does already. I like it smooth and silky. He likes it now too. He had so little body hair anyway it was easy for him. He also likes the silky dress pants and shirts I've been getting him."

"See, he's on the way and you didn't even know it. Now just keep it going."

Cole looked at me and smiled a wide grin.

"Cole, that doesn't mean you're gonna get to do me you know! I love my Jessie and would never do anything to hurt him."

"If you love him, you'll help him to feel good about himself by helping him become your girlfriend. Trust me."

"Yea right!"

I hopped off the treadmill and did my weights where Cole couldn't be near me enough to talk. He did his weights and I looked over to the side from time to time. I saw his bulging biceps lift the weight as his flat abs tensed and showed the six-pack beneath his tight tank top. His powerful thighs clenched as he pushed. Thighs I could imagine sitting on as I rode him. I finished my sets and went into the showers. When I came out Cole was toweling his thick black hair.

"Trust me. He'd love it. You could even help him make a few bucks turning tricks with the guys that frequent this place. A lot of them would pay dearly for a gal like Jessie."

I looked at Cole with a shocked look and my mouth open and tossed the gym bag over my shoulder. I walked out fishing my keys out of the side pocket. I drove home thinking about whether Jessie would really get into such a thing but I decided he probably wouldn't so I wouldn't push it. If it was true and these were things he wanted deep inside it would make him much happier and content with himself. I should have studied sexual problems more in school.

I pulled up our driveway to our secluded love nest. No one could see in our windows or see us in the yard or see us on the deck or anywhere on our property. Every time I pulled in I felt relaxed. As I approached, Jessie was in the driveway in his shorts bent over as he washed the bottom of the door of his Aston Martin DB9. A true gentlemen's car. Four hundred eighty horsepower but rides like a cloud. The James Bond car.

His bottom, as he bent over like that, struck me that it could be that of a thin woman's. His shapely legs were tanned and smooth. He turned to face me now with his bare chest showing his muscle tone. He didn't work out or anything but he got plenty of exercise around the house just doing things. He was always doing things and he stayed in good shape. Not huge muscles at all but firm and lean.

His long blond hair was now down across his shoulders with no ponytail to contain it. Any woman would envy the flow of his shiny waves. The sun sparkled off the silver studs in each of his ears. We were lucky to work where we did where people didn't care about guys wearing hair like that, or earrings either. He came over to me as I rolled down my window and smiled with his soft lips, smooth skin and white teeth.

"Hi sweetie! Leave your car out and I'll wash it for you while you make lunch. How's that for a deal!" Jessie said happily in a voice I now realized would also pass as a woman's. I couldn't stop thinking about seeing him that way now.

"Good deal baby. I'll make us something yummy." I couldn't help stopping to look back at him and think about how he'd look dressed as a woman. Na! He'd hate the idea. It would kill his ego altogether. His ego was the key as it most always is in psychiatric issues. I had to take care of his ego. He'd be much happier for it and then, maybe, just maybe, I could get to feel some man cock in me like in the movies. It would be worth a try that's for sure! I'm always willing to try and take a risk. Heck, how else do you get anything you want?

Breaching The Subject

Jenna had gotten back from the gym and I finished washing her Audi R8. A powerful woman's car. Men love it too but it fits her well. Powerful, fast, gorgeous, just like her. We had it good. I put both cars into the garage and went inside.

Jenna had lunch ready. She changed into her pink satin tank and short shorts. Her perky breasts pushed against the fabric and her nipples showed hard like they always did after her workout day. I think the exercise helped get her aroused since she was every time she came home from the gym on Sundays.

She stood holding my chair for me. "Here you go Jessie! Chilled cracked crab, avocado and mango. Mmm."

I sat at the table as she pushed in my chair. "Thanks sweetie! What's with holding my chair?"

"Oh, ha, I didn't even think about it. Just being nice I guess. Why, don't you like that?"

"Well, it kinda made me feel like I was the gal and you the guy."

"Oh, sorry."

Jenna was kind of quiet as we ate. The meal was awesome and perfect for a comfortable summers day. We ate, cleaned up and took some fresh lemonade out on the deck with us. The next part of the Sunday routine was something else I loved. Jenna laid a beach towel on the lounge chair and aimed it for the sun to be on her straight on. She peeled off her shorts and top and slipped out of her panties. She positioned herself on the lounge chair and held her hands out to me while she smiled, her long nails aching to be in my hair.

I knelt down on a towel before her, stripped myself naked to catch the sun on my back. I lowered my head between her legs and had my desert as she wrapped her fingers in my hair and held my head tight as I ate. I flicked her and ran circles around her and dove my tongue inside tasting her sweet smelling nectar. She writhed in pleasure and I throbbed in my shorts as she did. Jenna had orgasm after orgasm. I counted seven this time before she pulled my head up and licked my face clean then kissed me deeply. She rolled over on her belly and I lay down on the lounge chair beside her on my back.

We sunned for another half an hour listening to the big woodpeckers yapping away and the hawks screeching above as they circled. Jenna kissed me on the head and got me up so I wouldn't burn. We went in the shade on the couch swing and sat down and drank our lemonade.

"That was incredible as usual Jessie. Thank you!"

"You're welcome! My pleasure, trust me!"

"You like to see me pleased don't you."

"Love it more than anything Jenna."

"I love you and I love to see you pleased too. Do you like the new silky clothes and missile thong I got you?"

"Oh yea, those feel good."

"I think you should try on some women's clothes sometimes for me. I think you'd look really sexy in them."

"Really!? Na, I couldn't do that. I'd feel like an idiot."

"Why? Who would know, tell me."

"Well, no one really, but I'd know and then I'd feel really stupid and insignificant."

"What if I said I'd never think you were stupid or insignificant and I'd like to see if you liked it? I think it's just your male ego getting in the

14

way of you experiencing something not many men would be man enough to experience."

"Jessie, I think I'd feel silly. As a matter of fact, I've been thinking about cutting my hair again. About like your length, but a guys cut. I think it would make me more masculine looking and maybe look taller too."

"Cut your hair! Oh no please Jessie! I love it! Not many men can have hair as nice as yours. It's thick and blond and shiny and healthy looking. You look like a god with that hair!"

"It's a lot of work!"

"I know it is but please don't get rid of it. Your earrings wouldn't look as good if you did either."

"I was thinking of not wearing them either."

Jenna gave me her pouty lip and doe eyes. I couldn't resist.

"Okay, you win. I won't cut it and won't get rid of my earrings. But dressing as a woman is definitely out okay?"

"Okay."

Jenna leaned her head on my shoulder and dozed off for a nap. I had to think about what she said though. I did sometimes think I'd make a better girl than a man. But what a jerk I'd feel like then!

The Clothes Make The Man Not

I lay there with my head on Jessie's shoulder thinking. How could I do this? He'd never agree. He did shave his body and he did like silky men's clothes. Maybe I could introduce it in bed where he isn't so self-conscious. I decided that would be the start. I got up from the swing and took Jessie's hand. "Let's go shopping for some sexy clothes, what do you say?"

"All right! I love getting you sexy clothes."

Jessie put on some jeans and I put on some super sheer suntan thigh highs with a short denim skirt with four-inch wedge heels and a tight tank top. I had him wear a missile thong again so I could see if he got aroused. Jessie drove his car. I loved the smoothness and the power of it as we went through the back roads to the mall.

Jessie put his hand on my stocking clad leg as he drove and slid it up and down caressing me.

"Feels nice doesn't it? Think how nice these would feel on your legs. Then I could rub your legs like that too and I could feel how nice they feel. Why would you deny me that?"

"Oh Jenna, please."

I looked at his crotch and saw him throb when I said that.

"Just wishing a little, that's all. Remember, don't let your male ego get in the way of enjoying things."

We got to the mall and I took the lead taking Jessie to Victoria's Secret where I secretly bought things for him and a few for me. He didn't notice the slight difference in sizes or the fact that I had bought some bras in his size.

Then we went to a men's shoe store so I could see what size would be a good women's shoe size for Jessie. I had him measure his foot on the measuring thing and read the women's size at the same time. He was only a women's seven, two sizes bigger than me. He went to look at the men's shoes while I bought two pairs of women's shoes for him in the hopes I could get him to wear them sometime too. He didn't notice I had two pairs of each style that I bought since he was shopping for men's shoes. He found a pair he liked, interestingly, they were somewhat femininely styled.

We went into a juniors shop and I loaded up on more stuff for him and some for me, then the earring shop and perfume place. We dragged it all home.

Forced to Dress and Fantasize

Jenna took me for a romp through the mall and bought all kinds of hot clothes. I couldn't wait to see her in them. Jenna put them away and came down in one of the outfits. She wore a black baby doll nightgown and black five inch heeled pumps with gold dangling earrings and a gold necklace.

"Your turn Jessie. I put your clothes on the bed. Go put them on okay?" She smiled evily. Something was up.

I got upstairs and she had a pair of pantyhose and some short satin pants with a black satin shirt out. There was a pair of high heels there too. I got hard immediately as I thought about putting them on but thought about how silly I'd look. I opened the package of pantyhose and Jessie had cut out the crotch so my cock could be free. Hmm, a woman wouldn't wear pantyhose like that right? These were okay.

I slipped them on the way I had seen Jenna do it so many times. I rolled them to the toe then worked them up each leg stretching them as I pulled them up. I felt a rush of sensation as they slid silkily up my legs. I was rock hard. I slipped the black satin short shorts on, buttoned them tight and adjusted the belt. They felt nice. I slipped on the black satin shirt. I tried the shoes on but I felt silly and stuffed them under the bed. I went downstairs.

Jenna was smiling at me as she saw I had put some of the things on. "What? No shoes? Your legs would look so hot in those shoes."

"Sorry, couldn't do it."

"Okay. I like the stockings. Come here so I can rub your legs."

I sat next to Jenna and she did rub my legs and it felt incredible. It felt so sexy and wild to me. What was wrong with me?!

"See how nice that feels? And all you had to do was overcome your male ego. And your legs look so sexy in them. I think you should wear them whenever we play, and maybe more often too. Or, maybe some gartered stockings or thigh highs. Ah see? I said gartered stockings and I saw you cock throb under those shorts."

"That was just a coincidence."

"I don't think so. Be honest with yourself Jessie. Okay, tomorrow we're supposed to go to work. We have lots of time off and should probably take a vacation and use some of it up but why don't we wait a while and think about what would be good to do for vacation. Tonight I think I want to please you and not play myself. I want you to enjoy coming without watching me. I've come enough lately."

"But that's one of the things I love the most is seeing you come! How will I come?"

"How about if I tell you a story while I make you come? But you can only come the way I say. I want you to learn yourself better okay?"

"How can I argue with coming any way. It's a deal."

"Okay, now, we need to eat dinner and then relax and go to bed. If you're good I'll let you come before we go to sleep. First though, you have to go upstairs and put on those shoes and then we'll cook dinner together."

"Do I have to?"

"Only if you want to come. So, let go of that male ego and go put them on for me okay?"

I reluctantly did as I was told and struggled my way back down the stairs. I entered the kitchen as I wobbled and held on to the counters.

Jenna stopped and stood back to look at my legs as I tried to stand straight. "Awesome, I was right! You have gorgeous legs and those shoes do them wonders. Look at them and tell me they don't make you hot. They make me hot!"

I looked down and as she said, they were hot. Before I looked up Jenna was on her knees unzipped my shorts and sucked my cock looking up at me. The sight of her painted lips and big eyes looking up and my stockinged legs in heels was a strange combination but terribly exciting. She sucked and caressed me with her hot mouth and tongue until she got me to the edge of coming and then stopped. She tucked me back in and stood.

Jenna left the kitchen and ran up the stairs then came back down. She had a flared black leather mini skirt in her hands. "Take those shorts off and put this on. It's black leather and manly like a kilt. If I'm gonna be able to suck that cock I need to get to it easier. And I don't want to hurt it on your pants zipper. This will be better."

"What? Put on a skirt? No way! I'd feel like a jerk!"

"See, there goes that male ego again. Come on now, this is a very rugged looking skirt and your pantyhose have a hole cut in them for a cock. What women have a cock to put through a hole in their pantyhose. Put that male ego aside and enjoy the spoils of listening to me or don't come tonight and don't feel hot and sexy. If you aren't going to do it you can forget about coming for another week and go change into some boring male clothes."

Jenna looked at me as if she meant business. I could see how she was such a high up boss. Not coming for a whole week would be hell and she'd figure out how to have it happen too. Probably some kind of chastity cage or something.

She stood there waiting for my reply then she spoke. "Yes, I would put a chastity cage on you. Remember the one I showed you to stop you from jerking off in the bathroom when I wasn't around? I never had to use it because I could tell if you came or not by the way you'd act but trust me I would use it now. I only want to help you be happy and feel good and I want you to have some patience with me and try this out. Baby, I love you."

There she goes combining toughness with love and I couldn't resist it. I took off the shorts and slid on the black leather skirt and zipped it up the back. I felt my cock lift in the air beneath it and rub against the lining. I felt silly.

"Good job honey. You'll see, you'll love this. Let's make dinner."

We always did as many things together as possible since we always wanted to be in each other's company. Making dinner was always pleasant, though I liked to cook more than Jenna, and I was actually a better cook. Jenna was chopping vegetables and I had a thought.

"Jenna, why don't you let me cook while you go dress for dinner? I mean, for me if that's okay. You know, since I like to cook more and well, you had me dress like this, how about if you just put on a sexy cocktail dress for me and then we'll eat? Please?"

"Okay sweetie. But I'm not going to come for you okay?"

"Aww, but, okay."

I felt myself get aroused thinking of seeing Jenna dressed in a little cocktail dress and heels and then thought about how I was dressed. Between the two, I felt aroused and excited about actually doing this. I sat on the kitchen chair and crossed my legs. I felt what it felt like to have stockings, high heels and a skirt on. Sitting down like that had an erotic feel to it. I crossed and uncrossed my legs and ran my hands over the stockings. I ran a hand over the front of the skirt and felt my cock hard and slipping under the skirt. I thought about Jenna on her knees sucking my cock by simply lifting my skirt. Wow! She was right so far.

This was pretty cool. I stood up with my hard on and felt the walk my heels gave me as I walked around the kitchen making dinner with my hard cock rubbing against the skirt all the time. It brought me to a new level of riding the edge of coming without even using my hands.

I made us some angel hair pasta in clam sauce with artichoke hearts and asparagus. I paired it with a light, floral bouquet Riesling. When Jenna came down I had just set the table and dinner was ready. I sat in the chair and unconsciously slid one leg over the other as I sat with them crossed. I bounced my one dangling foot in its high heel shoe. I could feel my thighs press on my cock as it slid between my stockinged thighs. I was stared off into the distance and sipped the wine as I did. I heard Jenna speak and she took me from the other world I had been in.

"Ah, yes! See Jessie? I knew you'd enjoy that! From now on this is how you shall dress after work."

Jenna sat at the table slipping her long nailed hands under her hot pink mini dress before she sat. She crossed her luscious legs in the suntan pantyhose and now I knew how it felt to her as she did so and felt myself throb once more as I stood to put dinner on the table. I walked in minced steps to the stove and back as Jenna poured herself a glass of wine and watched me walk.

"Very nice Jessie. You've now gotten the walk down. See, it wasn't so hard was it? And I know your cock is hard and feeling nice. Just put one foot in front of the other but a little to the opposite side and the walk will fell sexier yet."

I did as she said and it did feel even sexier as it made my hips move more dramatically. I caught my heel and almost dropped the plates of food but righted myself. "Oops, almost, see, I shouldn't be doing this. It's not natural."

"Jessie, there is nothing natural about putting pencils on your heels and trying to walk on them. Every woman has to learn it as will you."

I put the plates down, seated myself by slipping my hand under my skirt as I had seen Jenna do.

"Very nice Jessie. I will reward you well for being such a good student. Thanks for the wonderful smelling meal too!" Jenna blew me a kiss from her seat and we both dug in.

"Now Jessie, try to eat like you're wearing a skirt not pants. It will make it feel more natural to you." Jenna held a fork out showing me how I should hold it more femininely. I copied that and then she lifted her wine glass to drink and I copied that. She dabbed her lips with her napkin and I copied that. "Very good! I'm so proud of you being a man and stepping up to this! Let's eat!"

Jenna and I ate our meals quickly while I practiced what she had shown me, Jenna said I should make us some coffee and she would be in the great room watching TV while I cleaned up the kitchen. I did as I was told and got wrapped up in the sensations of what I was wearing so much that I think I cleaned the kitchen three times, rewashing the counters and cleaning the sink. When I got to the great room, Jenna had the big dildo and was coming on it as she watched the video we watched the other night. She finished coming just as I entered.

"I thought you weren't going to come? Why didn't you wait for me?" I whined and heard myself sound so pitiful.

"I'm sorry but you got me so hot thinking about where we might go with this that I had to relieve myself so I could pay attention to you." Jenna handed me the cock so I could wash it and put it away. Now go upstairs and put away my cock and put on the clothes I left on the bed for you. I want you to wear them when you come tonight. If you don't, well, I don't need to come anymore and so I guess we'd be done. If you do, I promise you a story and a come to remember." She grinned and smiled at me as she was wiping the wetness off the leather couch with a towel.

I went upstairs and washed her cock, disappointed that I missed seeing her use it. I put it away in the bag and went over by the bed where she had laid out a complete set of clothing. I started with the stockings. She had gartered, suntan, extra, extra, sheer stockings. I felt them and one caught on an insignificant piece of dry cuticle on my hand. I decided I had to make sure my legs were perfectly shaved and toenails sanded so I didn't ruin them. I had to ask Jenna if it was okay.

"Jenna," I shouted from upstairs. "These stockings are so sheer I think I should shave again and file my toenails so they don't run them. Is that okay?"

Jenna yelled back at me, "It's only six o'clock so sure, we have plenty of time. That's a great idea! Do that and shave your chest and your face too in case there is a little stubble. I'll come up and help you when I hear the water stop."

I showered and shaved what little soft stubble there was on my body since I didn't have much body hair anyway. Then I cut and filed my toenails and fingernails so they wouldn't catch on the stockings. When I was done Jenna showed up in the bathroom.

"Sit here on the makeup chair facing away from the mirror and let me have a look at you."

I sat on a towel naked before her as she scrutinized my face and body and ran her hands through my hair. "Yes, yes yes, Okay, now be patient with me I need to do a few things."

Jenna took a pair of tweezers and started to quickly tweeze my eyebrows.

"Hey what are you doing? I don't want thin eyebrows."

"Oh don't be silly, I'm not gonna make them real real thin. Just neaten them up some. I think they call it manscaping." She did this for a few minutes then she came at me with an eyeliner.

"What? Eyeliner? Oh Jenna please."

"Hush, it washes right off." Then she took the eyeliner and lined my eyes followed by mascara. Eye shadow followed along with a sheer foundation and blush. She lined my lips with a lip pencil and then filled them in with lipstick on a brush. A spot of lip gloss went in the center of my lower lips and on the center of the top. I could smell the smells of the makeup and thought how silly I was going to look. I was happy I wasn't watching in the mirror She stood back and looked at me.

Jenna then put some makeup on my chest. A light color located just around the inside of my boobs as if I had any. "I do this too, it makes them appear to stand out more. You'll see." Jenna then took her body powder and dipped the puff and had me stand so she could cover me with it. I smelled like Jenna and felt silky. She took a quick-dry nail polish out of the drawer and masterfully painted my toenails. Watching her do that and seeing my feet transformed made my maleness swell for some reason.

She looked up seeing the motion of it in her peripheral vision. "See? I told you you'd love this. Just wait till we're done baby."

Jenna finished my toenails and did my fingernails.

"Hey! I have to go to work tomorrow!"

"Don't worry, well go in a little late and you'll have time to take it off." Jenna held my hand and painted all my nails. I could feel the coolness of the polish evaporating on each nail as she stroked it on They looked so stubby next to Jenna's. "We'll have to get you some nice false nails like mine so you can feel how good they feel. That's for another time though." Jenna stood and took me by the hand into the bedroom to help me dress. It was obvious she was on a mission and Jenna always gets what she wants so I stopped arguing.

I leaned against the bed as I took the stockings and slid them one at a time up my leg and they quickly began to slide back down. Jenna commented, "You have to have the garter belt on first or you'll have to do it all over again. That's okay Jessie you'll learn." She reached around me, wrapped the garter belt around my waist and hooked it and then she got on her knees, sucked my cock, brought me to the edge of an orgasm and stopped. "See how good these things feel? Now attach the garters."

I slid the stockings back up carefully feeling the gossamer thin fabric caress my smooth skin. I tried to attach them. I struggled with the clasps until Jenna showed me the proper way to attach them. Jenna had me put my black strappy high heels back on. Jenna then took the bra and showed me how to hold it and clasp it in front and then rotate it around and slip my arms in the straps. She adjusted the straps for me. "I'll adjust these but you'll learn where to set them for each different bra. We'll get you something to fill the bras too later since this is just for feel more than show right now." Jenna reached inside the bra and pulled what flesh I had in so that the part she made up did look like it popped out some. It was as if I had an B cup even with the illusion it created.

Jenna put long dangling gold earrings in my ears removing all four of my studs and placing them on the dresser. She then brushed my hair.

She had me lean over and she brushed and fluffed my hair and sprayed some hairspray on it while I was upside down. She held me down till it dried some and then lifted me up. She brushed it lightly and put a pair of gold clips on each side holding back the front hairs to sweep across my face.

She then tied a black ribbon in the back of my hair and fluffed up my curls spraying them again. Next she sprayed me all over with her perfume. I was now enveloped in my favorite scent. She stood back and looked at me with a satisfied smile.

"You're gorgeous! Sooo hot. Mmmm. I think I could come looking at you. Look in the mirror now."

I stood in front of the mirror and couldn't believe my eyes!!! My face and eye makeup were incredible! The bra and garter belt with the stockings and high heels looked like they were meant for me. I didn't have much of a butt or boobs but I did look like a slim woman and NOT like a man. That is, until I saw my cock throbbing in the air and so did Jenna.

"Oh look! Your cock is dancing it's so happy!" Jenna turned me sideways so I could still look in the mirror as she lovingly suckled my cock bringing me to riding the edge of an orgasm for a good five minutes. My skin tingled and my body felt alive with vibration as she masterfully held me at that point of bliss. I was about to come when Jenna stopped and stood. "Okay now the panties and the dress. I think the black crotchless panties will work nice with that dress letting you be free under the bubble hem."

Jenna held the panties for me to step into as I put my hand on her shoulder to balance. Then she held the dress for me to step in and I pulled it up. She arranged the straps of the leopard print, bubble hem, mini dress to best show my minimal cleavage that she made. Jenna adjusted the hem so it was a little shorter and puffier and I could feel the silky fabric against the tip of my drooling cock. Jenna sprayed perfume on me once more and put it in a purse. "Here, a lady always has a purse." She handed it to me.

She went to the dresser and put a woman's gold watch on my arm and a bracelet on the other along with a gold necklace around my neck. She walked me over to the mirror again. My senses were fully alive feeling all the sensations on my skin and smelling the perfume. I heard the birds outside at the feeder and saw the crisp green of the trees through the window. My skin tingled all over and I felt like I had been reborn. How would I ever deny this now?

"Look, look at the woman you are!"

I looked and was overwhelmed. So much so I felt faint and heard the rush of blood through my body as my heart raced. Jenna sensed it.

"Are you okay? You need to sit?"

"Phew, I'm okay, it's just, it's just such a shock. Maybe I never really was a man? Maybe I was supposed to be a woman and things got messed up?" The sight of myself was so overwhelming, I felt like I was going to cry and held it back.

Jenna kissed me gently on the cheek so as to not mess my makeup and she stroked my shoulders. "It's okay baby, I love you this way. You can now be my life partner, spouse, and girlfriend too! It's okay. Let's go relax downstairs now."

Jenna took me by the hand as she gently led me down stairs. She took me outside on the path on our property and we walked in the woods and gardens following it. I felt better now and once more became immersed in the sensations. Everything was so much more intense this way. I felt the path beneath my shoes and heard each step as we both clicked our heels walking. I practiced one foot ahead of the other and slightly to the other side and felt my hips obey, wagging my butt. I felt my cock as it was in its splendor beneath the bubble hem feeling the tip caressed by the fabric with each step. I felt Jenna's hand in mine and ran my finger over her nails feeling their smoothness and how graceful and long her nails were.

"Yes, you can and will have nails like that too." She nuzzled her head against me and swung my arm. "Wooh HOO!!!! She yelled at the top of her lungs. "I have a girlfriend to play with!!" Jenna skipped and hopped and made me do the same as we made our way along the path.

We climbed the steps and sat on the bench on the stone patio out back of the great room. Jenna leaned into me and rubbed me through the dress bringing me to the edge once more. We kissed carefully and I felt our lipstick-covered lips sensually caress each other as our tongues danced. Jenna took my cock between her two fingers and her thumb using the fabric of the dress to stroke me in. My breath quickened and she stopped. "Okay, let's go inside sister."

Jenna stood and led the way as I watched her beautiful bottom swish back and forth in the tight pink lycra dress. We entered through the French doors and Jenna led us into the kitchen as I paid attention to her walk and imitated it.

"Drink? How about something pretty. Maybe a peach mango martini with a strawberry garnish and a straw!"

"Sounds different!"

"A pretty drink for a pretty girl! Go sit in the great room and I'll bring it in."

I walked into the great room thoroughly enjoyed everything about this, and felt like I had had an epiphany. I seated myself on the leather sofa and felt the cool smoothness against my thighs and bottom. I adjusted my dress beneath me and crossed my legs. I bounced my foot once more and enjoyed the feel of it all. I reached in my purse and sprayed some perfume between my knees and on my wrist. I turned on the television and flipped through the channels. I stopped at the fashion channel enthralled with the woman modeling.

"Here you are sweetie. I made a pitcher of them so we wouldn't have to get up so much and I got your lipstick and smokes for your purse. And here is the other half of that pill for you. I don't think I need to see if you're getting aroused or not, I know you are so let's make it good and hard."

Jenna poured two martinis and put the garnish and straws in them. She put the smokes and a lighter in my purse along with my lipstick and lip-gloss. I had to check and see if it was okay from our kissing so I went to the bathroom, checked it and reapplied it and managed to do a good job of it. I seated myself once more alongside my gorgeous wife.

"I love you Jenna," I said as I ran my hand over her silken leg while seating myself.

"I love you too baby. Thanks for doing this for me! You look so good!" Jenna and I sipped our martinis and I took the pill while she rubbed my thighs through the stockings again, which felt incredible! We sipped and watched the show. I had to comment on everything about the clothes they tried on. I opened my purse and lit a cigarette and when I put it in the ash tray I saw my lipstick making those slutty marks on the filter and I felt like I was a slutty woman myself. I throbbed between my crossed legs.

"Like the way you leave that lipstick stain on it huh? Me too."

Jenna went upstairs and came back down with another set of bra, panties and garter belt along with a matching camisole. They were pink lace and satin. She held them out showing them to me. "This is what you will wear to work under your clothes tomorrow. I thought you should see how pretty they are and feel how nice they feel."

Jenna knelt before me again and lifted my dress. She took my cock between one finger and her thumb and ran the fabric of each item over it. She stroked me and brought me to the edge over and over with them. I twitched from time to time as she ran it over the tip and rubbed them on the head.

"See how nice these feel? Tomorrow and every day from now on you'll wear pretty things to work under your man clothes." She stroked me with them and caressed me some more. She seated herself next to me and rubbed my legs as well as caressed my cock with those clothes. "Just watch your show sweetie and enjoy some more martini and a smoke. Let me make you feel good."

I watched as the fashion show continued and my loving wife took care of me making me feel incredible. My E.D. pill had kicked in and I was like a rock.

I went to the bathroom and I had to struggle to go pee by pushing it down and thinking about baseball. I managed and stood up after I adjusted my garter straps and slipped the crotchless panties back around my once more rock solid maleness. I fixed my lipstick and put on more perfume. I wondered if I'd be able to fuck Jenna and then thought again that it was a bad idea since I'd only come in seconds and she'd be left wanting more. I went back into the room and we sat, drank, smoked and Jenna held me at the edge for the next hour.

We went to bed at ten o'clock and Jenna had me get in bed dressed as I was. She had me pull my legs back with my heels by my hips. She used the clothing I'd wear tomorrow to stroke my cock. She whispered into my ear as she stroked. "Would you like to see me get fucked by a big cock?"

"Yes, please!"

"No not a dildo, I want you to imagine me getting fucked like the girls on the porn video. Can you do that?"

Could I do that? Of course I could. That's how I jerked off before Jenna stopped me from doing it without her. "I uh, think I can."

"Okay, the story starts at a bar we both go to together. You're dressed as you are and I as I am. We both dance with each other and you're hard beneath your dress reveling in all the wonderful sensations. We have a few drinks and dance and some guys find us and buy us drinks. That's okay for two girls to do right?"

"Of course," I say as I feel the tension growing in me.

"The guys want to have a smoke so we all go outside and have one with them. The one with you puts his big hand on your ass through your dress and you feel how good it feels."

"Mmm, weird but not bad."

"The one I'm with does the same to me. Of course you see it and your happy to know how good it feels to me because you've felt it too."

"Yes, I feel as if I'm you."

"Good, The guy you're with takes your long fingernailed hand and puts it on his crotch so you can feel how big and hard he is. His friend does the same to me. Can you see it? Close your eyes and see it all."

I closed my eyes, trying to imagine it. The fabric of the clothes Jenna gently stroked me with felt so nice on my cock. "Yes, I see it. I'll have to do something to keep from having the guy with me find out my secret."

"Yes you will. What might distract him?"

"Maybe I should rub his cock since I have my hand on it. But I'm a guy!"

"You're not a guy! And yes, that will work for a while. Do you see what the guy with me is doing now?"

"Yes, he has his fingers inside of you and your kissing him while you unzip his pants."

"Very good Jessie. What might happen next? What is the guy you are with trying to do?"

"Oh my God! He's trying to finger me! I squat down so as to not get my knees dirty and I unzip his pants and take his cock out and stroke it."

"Good thinking girl! That's better, now he can't reach your secret. What is happening with me?"

"You have a huge cock, like the ones in the movies, in your hand and your hand looks tiny on it. He takes his hand out of you and it's soaking wet. You pull him closer to you and lift your leg alongside his hip. I see your hand guide his huge cock into you and I see your eyes roll back in your head. He starts pounding into you banging you against the brick wall of the building!"

"What is your guy doing now?"

"He's getting really hot watching you two and he grabs my head putting his cock in front of my lips and pushes it. I have to take it in."

Jenna took the middle size dildo and slipped it into my mouth moving it in and out while she continued to stroke my cock with tomorrow's clothes. "Oh my god! He's fucking me so hard. I'm coming on his cock. It feels so fucking good. I'm so full and wet! Ungh, Ungh fuck me baby! The guy in your mouth comes while you look at me from the corner of your eye!"

I felt myself well up and ran my tongue over the dildo as I came violently as Jenna stroked my cock. I saw her in my mind's eye getting laid fabulously. I felt her release the dildo while I continue to suck it and her hand caught my come in the palm. I felt myself still coming after there was no more come and I felt the dildo now pull out and reenter my mouth with my come on it. My body released all its tension and I suddenly felt very tired.

"Aww yes, nice job baby! That was an awesome come you had wasn't it? See how nice those fantasies can be?"

"Mmm," was all I could say. I fell off to sleep not waking till the next morning.

New Rules and Watching My Wife

"Wake up sleepy head!" Jenna said as she dove down on my dick and sucked my morning hard on. "Mmm, love that little cock of yours. You take a shower and shave and such and I'll make breakfast for you and get your clothes ready."

"No girl's underwear!"

"Yes girl's underwear! No one will know. Plus, I want you to jerk off at work at lunch and any other time you feel you need to in order to concentrate. I have a thing for you to capture it all in so it's not wasted too. Now of course, you could NOT wear the clothes I want you to and we can NOT play this anymore. If you're good, and do what I say, we can have a little party every night when we go to bed. Otherwise the next time we play is next weekend, uh, maybe."

I looked at her as I stood in my outfit from last night and she kneeled before me, sucked my cock again and brought me to the edge for a good fifteen minutes. She looked up. "Keep playing the game or, should I put a cock cage on you to wear to work. Hmmm, cock cage or pretty clothes. You decide."

"Pretty clothes."

"Go get washed up. Don't forget to change the earrings you have on back to your studs and to wash the makeup off. You can practice putting it on yourself tonight." Jenna went downstairs and made breakfast. I did all my morning rituals along with removing makeup and fingernail polish but left the toenail polish on. It did make my feet look sexy. I dressed in the clothes she used to make me come last night under my regular clothes. It felt very strange.

I went downstairs and ate breakfast with Jenna. She was wearing her usual power suit style with a fairly short mini skirt about four inches above the knee and a push up bra. She wore her gartered stockings as usual. Her hair was gelled as usual. She looked gorgeous and powerful as she stood and drank her coffee as she looked at me in thought.

Jenna went into the freezer and took out a small thermos, very small. "Here, this is a medical thermos for keeping medications fresh. I've frozen it so it will keep anything in it cool all day. I want you to come in this anytime you want to during the day. Now don't waste any because I have plans for it. She handed it to me. It was about the size of my cock, well, maybe a little smaller. It was about three inches long and one inch around. I put it in my back jeans pocket. We went to work with Jenna driving her R8.

The day dragged on for me. I couldn't stop thinking about what had happened and how it made me feel. At first, I felt pretty silly with the underwear and stockings on and being able to feel it all but, after I noticed that no one else noticed it actually felt nice and kinda like Jenna's and my secret.

That was when I began to relax. I'd crossed my legs and felt the stockings, I'd leaned back and I felt the pull of the bra. I'd get distracted from my programming and have to shut the door on my office and jerk off so I could get back to work. I ended up coming more than I ever did in a day and by the time the day ended I had nearly filled the container half way. At first I thought I'd miss the container but it fit the head of my dick so well it actually made it feel better using it than not. I wondered what Jenna would say since she hadn't let me come by myself in so long and now she wanted me to. Jenna came by my office and picked me up on the way out.

"What do you say we go to dinner before we go home? I don't feel like cooking unless you want to cook by yourself."

"Go out with me dressed like this?"

"Of course, no one will know what you're doing. We could snuggle in the back booth of the restaurant and then maybe if I gave you a few drinks I could get you to dress up and make you come," Jenna said with smiling pleading eyes.

"Hmm. Ply me with a few drinks so you can take advantage of me. Sounds interesting. Let's go."

Jenna drove once more and when she got out for the valet he nearly popped his eyes out looking at her. He held her hand and helped her out. When he did, the tops of her stockings showed as well as a good view of her breasts as the blouse hung forward.

"Enjoy your meal ma'am," he said as he took one last look at her before getting in the driver's seat.

"Jenna, he sure got an eyeful. You should have seen the look on his face."

"I know, isn't it great the way women have such power over men? Did you mind him looking at me?"

"Of course not. I have you and he doesn't. I rather like showing you off. You know that."

"Of course, just checking." Jenna took my hand, we walked inside Jenna discretely handed a twenty to the host and we were seated at a booth in the back. Jenna had me sit first and then she slid in next to me pushing us around until we were at the back. The long tablecloth hid the fact that Jenna had her hand on my crotch as the waiter took our drink orders. Jenna ordered me a long island iced tea and a mango martini for herself.

"Okay Jessie. Let me see the thermos." She stuck her other hand out palm up.

"Here ya go. I was, uh a little distracted today."

Jenna opened it and looked inside. "Are you sure you didn't put other stuff in here too? That is a lot of come!" She whispered and laughed.

"Nope nothing else. I was surprised I didn't dry up."

"How many times? Did you count them?"

I thought about it and counted on my fingers. I came up with four times at work. "Four at work I think."

"Very good! I want you to try for more each day. Maybe if you had a video of me coming or something that would help?"

Jenna's hand was squeezing my cock through my pants and panties. "From that hard throb, I think that was a yes. Well, this dressing like this and coming so much today certainly hasn't tainted your desire any. You're like, ready to get it on baby." She smiled and kissed me as the drinks arrived. While the waiter was putting them down she unzipped my fly using both hands. He had to see that. Then she took me out of my pants and took a pair of pink satin panties out of her purse on the table. She took them under the table and wrapped them around me. I know he saw them go under the table and he had to know what she was doing. Her arm moved against my bicep as she looked at the waiter smiling as she jerked me off! It was obvious he saw as his eyes darted around nervously.

"Uh, ready to order or would you like some time to uh, build up an appetite." He grinned now as he watched my wife jerk me off and I smiled and winked at him as I sat back confidently and put my arms on the booth's back.

Jenna ordered for both of us and the waiter left.

"Are you crazy? Are you trying to get us thrown out of here?" I said as Jenna continued to stroke me.

"Oh shush. He's gonna do no such thing. How does it feel to have a hot, sexy, powerful woman jerk you off like this in public while you wear all those girlie clothes underneath?"

"Quite good actually. I admit I was embarrassed for a moment and then thought I should not be and it would go better."

"That was a good choice and one you should remember. It's your male ego that is going to keep getting uncomfortable with what we're doing. But you have to be a man about it. What does a man do when he has fear?" Jenna stroked me faster now.

"He faces it of course."

"Right, so you can't be afraid of the way you feel when you dress like a woman or act like one. If you are, you'd only be showing me that you aren't really a man correct?"

"Uh, I guess." I had to stop Jenna before I came.

"Last night you faced your fears and what happened?"

"Uh, it was really good."

"Right! And I have a feeling it will continue to be." Jenna started stroking me again slowly then. She slid the fabric loosely against me. She looked me in the eyes. "Would you like to see me do this to someone else while you watched? I mean, would that be a fun fantasy too?"

I shuddered and I had to hurry to take Jenna's hand off before I came with that statement.

"I'll take that as a yes. Of course you'd like to see me in action like that, so much better than me playing with toys for you. You could even video me with your phone while I did and then maybe you can come six times at work instead of four. We'll use that in our fantasies then too. Sooo, Maybe we should go to bar after and I could put on a little show for you with some stranger we'll never see again. You could sit at the bar, imagine you're my girlfriend watching me and I could come in after and get some guy going. You could nonchalantly video it and then we could leave."

"Around here? What if someone we know sees?"

"If someone we know is there or comes in we'll just leave. I'll say I'm going to the ladies room and we go. O come on! You'll love it! You can jerk off to it all day tomorrow. Just make believe you're my girlfriend watching me."

"I don't know. Let's eat first okay?"

"Okay sweetie."

Well, Jenna and I ate our meals. I hardly know how either of us managed to eat with her stroking me so much but by the time we were done I had had three long island iced teas and she had two martinis and I had very little willpower when she asked me again if I wanted to go to a bar while she stroked me in those panties. I acquiesced. Jenna paid the bill and stuffed the panties in her purse along with my thermos.

Jenna drove us to a wild nightclub downtown where it was highly unlikely anyone we knew would be. It was known as a hot pickup joint for one night stands and had lots of out of town business travelers there. She gave me a parting comment before she ran ahead. "You're my girlfriend watching me right sweetie?" She winked at me.

Jenna went in first and I followed a distance behind her. She looked back to be sure I was following and I could tell she had selected the guy and the seat she would sit at. He was at a booth by himself with a table with a long tablecloth hanging down almost to the floor as all the other tables were. Now thinking about it, I see why the nightclub did that with the tablecloth.

He appeared to be about six foot four and had broad shoulders. He sipped a whiskey and ice and looked around. Jenna looked at me and shrugged her shoulders as a question. I nodded my head and looked for a seat at the bar where I could watch. I sat down and ordered a drink and by the time I did, this guy was up and getting Jenna a drink. He stood next to me and I could smell his cologne.

He had a shaved chest with gold chains and a thick gold watch. His white silk shirt was open to show the chains, his muscles and the hair on his chest. I dropped my napkin and bent down to pick it up and I saw he had a huge hardon in his silk pants. What was I doing! My wife was going to play with this guy! What if she couldn't get away? He took the drinks back to the table where Jenna was seated as she put on lipstick.

My heart was racing as I turned on my phone and put it on video reverse so I could point it behind me and as it turned on I could see Jenna's arm go beneath the table as she leaned forward and kissed the guy sucking his face. I was getting a perfect shot on the phone and held it as if I was reading something while I sipped my drink.

The guy squeezed her to him and put his hand under the table. I could tell that he had gotten under Jenna's skirt by the way she pushed against his hand egging him on. This went on for a while, some people passed and looked quickly and others didn't even notice. I had to cross my legs as I got hard watching and saw Jenna as she came hard on his hand while he groped her one breast and sucked her face. I could tell she came by the way her body moved as it always did when she came. She tensed up and went rigid as she pulled his hair on the back of his head.

They went on for a good ten minutes with her coming two more times on his hand. It seemed the more they got into it the less people paid attention. I lost any fear for Jenna as she took control now as usual.

She took the panties she used on me out of her purse and took them under the table. I saw her arm move in the motion that was familiar to me at dinner. The guy put his arms back on the booth like I did and sipped his drink as he watched her intently.

It wasn't more than a few minutes and I saw him tense up and push against the booth as Jenna's arm moved faster now. Then, he went limp. Jenna's both hands were now under the table. I assumed she was wiping him up and putting him away. The panties came up from under in a ball in her hand and went into her purse. She stood, kissed him and excused herself to go to the ladies room. She looked at me, smiled and winked as she passed by and I followed her out the back door to our car.

"Was that good Jessie? Pretty hot wasn't it? Did you come?"

"I was scared at first but I did what you said and I faced my fear and trusted in you to stay in control. I did almost come in my panties! It was very hot! You came three times on his hand! I never was able to get you to come with my hand. You were so hot to watch as you took control of him and had him finger you till you came over and over and then how you made him come after you were ready!! You have his come in those panties?"

"I love that you loved watching me do that. Watching me come so hard for you with a total strange hunk of a man. I have to tell you, honey, his hands are like his cock, big and hard and they reach all the right places so it was so easy for me to come. I was so excited that you were watching me too that it made me come faster than I would have. Oh yea, I have his come in the panties too. Oh yea, lots and lots, He had a huge amount. About five times as much as you ever shot! Just like his cock size, huge! They are soaked. I loved doing that for you." Jenna smiled with excitement at the accomplishment and she was so happy with how much it pleased me to see that. I have to admit, I did get powerfully excited watching her do it.

We got home and Jenna had me rinse off, dress and do my makeup. By then it was about eight o'clock and we needed to relax. Jenna put on a nightgown, the same as the one she had me dress in. I had the usual compliment of girlie lingerie underneath and I was anxious to come and fall asleep.

We watched some television and Jenna caressed my stockinged legs and my cock as we did. She commented on how I'd like to see this guy or that guy bang her and I'd get too excited thinking about it and I'd have to push her hand away. She sucked my cock for a while and then about nine thirty we went to bed.

Jenna had me jerk myself off, for her to watch, while she made me tell the story of what she did that night. Right before I was ready to come she stuck the medium dildo in my mouth. This time, she caught my come in a container and put it in the freezer again with the rest. I fell fast asleep.

She Put the Cage On Me!

This went on with going to dinner and coming home doing what we did for two weeks. And that was after a daily filling up of that thermos, and each day I came more! I came about twelve times a day in total now and could hardly stop myself. I had several videos on my phone of Jenna in bar booths jerking guys off and even four taken over the top of a stall in the men's room when she gave a guy a blowjob. It was then that I began to have second thoughts about how right this was or not. We were lying in bed falling asleep after I came with the dildo in my mouth as usual. Jenna even had me take one to work to suck when I watched her giving blowjobs on my phone.

"Jenna, I don't want to do this anymore. I want to go back and be what we were. It doesn't seem right. I think I should be a man."

"Be a man? How can you say that? When did you ever enjoy yourself so much?"

"Well, never really, but it just seems wrong."

"Seems wrong? You just said that you never really enjoyed yourself so much! Then who is judging what's right and wrong? We are two consenting adults in love and we're both enjoying this more than anything we've done sexually. No harm is coming to anyone just pleasure. What could possibly be wrong!? You're letting your paradigms and fears get you again. Some man! Okay, tomorrow you are back to what you were. But the cage is going on. No coming unless I let you. Since enjoying yourself is wrong then doesn't that seem appropriate?"

"Uh, okay."

The next morning I washed off my makeup, showered and got dressed in my normal man clothes and went downstairs. Jenna didn't have breakfast for me so I made some toast and butter and had some juice. After we were done in the bathroom after breakfast Jenna had me come into the bedroom as she stood there in a beige power suit.

"Drop your pants Jessie. I need to put this on." She held the chastity cage up. I dropped my pants reluctantly and she had me push my balls, one at a time, through the metal ring. She had chosen the smallest ring of the set so it wouldn't fall off. Next she had me push my cock through the ring above my balls. I slid the ring back as far as it would go feeling the cold hardness of it. Jenna then slid the cold metal cage over my cock and pushed it back till she could get it over the pin on the ring, get the pins on the cage aligned and into the ring and then she slipped the brass lock through the hole and clasped it with a click. She put the key in her purse. It was now locked in place and pulled on my cock and balls with the weight of it. It held my cock bent and restricted so I couldn't get a full hardon and would never be able to come but only pee.

I went to work each day like that for over a week. The weight of the cage was a constant reminder to me that I couldn't come. I would get hard and feel myself constricted inside of it and then get even harder until I could distract myself. After coming so many times for the last weeks I now was used to coming a lot and not coming was frustrating as hell! I was constantly aroused, squeezed against the steel of the cage, and wanted sex. I had even more thoughts about it then I did before. I'd try to shake the cage to make myself come and rub myself between the wires of it but it was no use. I remained horny as hell with no coming. I didn't even think of watching the videos of Jenna since that would only make things worse.

At night Jenna would put on videos and make me watch her come on her dildos. Then she would tell me she loved me and kiss me and fall fast asleep. I'd lie there tortured with that thing on until she released me to shower. She'd stay in there and watch me to make sure I didn't come. I was so horny.

The previous two weeks I had been coming a million times a day and now I hadn't come in over a week! I had been filling that entire thermos everyday and now it was all stuck inside of me. I didn't know what to do. She never even asked if I changed my mind. I honestly thought she would have us go on this way forever.

Was I wrong? Was Jenna wrong? I mean I'm no dummy either. I have a doctorate in software design but maybe my psychiatrist wife is right and I should listen to her. I did that for one more week through the time Jenna had her period, which was at least a relief that I didn't have to see her come when I couldn't. Then, I had to do something; I was going insane with desire. My libido was beyond nymphomaniac and this cage was the problem.

Deloto and Newgen

Being a Good Girl Means Freedom

"Jenna, honey, I think I was wrong. If you'd be willing, I'd like to go back to what we were doing."

"Really? Hmm I'm not so sure. I'd like to take you further with the feminine thing but it's gonna be a lot of work and I'm not sure you'll follow through. Having that freedom to come like you were has to be earned by doing certain things. I'd hate to waste my time and yours just to have you change your mind again. How can I know you're sure you want to be girlie again and not give up? How can I know you'll be my girlfriend as well as my life partner and spouse? How can I know? I'm not sure I want to bother. I'm not sure you're strong enough." Jenna went back to reading her book in bed while I lay there looking at the ceiling.

I thought about what she said and I didn't have a way to prove it to her. I just wanted the cage off, not necessarily by being girlie or watching her have sex with other men, though that was incredible to watch for some reason, but I knew she wouldn't let me do it any other way. "Honey, how can I prove it to you. I feel so apart from you now. I'm not even sure what to do. We could be partners in a new way of living. The way I was meant to be I guess like you say, a woman in all respects except one. I was wrong for stopping. You were right." I rolled over on my side facing away from Jenna.

I felt her hand on my shoulder. "Oh honey, it would be easy to convince me. Just agree with everything I say right now and I'll do it."

My wonderful wife was willing to try again. I sat up in bed, brushed my hair over my shoulder and looked at her. "Really? Aw thank you baby. I love you so much I'd do anything for you."

"Me too Jessie, me too. Okay, first I think we need to find a different first name for you since you associate Jessie with a male. Any suggestions?"

"Women's names. Hmm. I always liked Yvette but that's French."

"Yvette? That's an okay one. I like that. Yvette. Okay, you shall be called Yvette when in girl mode." Jenna reached over to her nightstand, took out the key to my chastity device and undid it. "Go put on a nightgown now and come back."

I put on a short pink nightgown with pink lace panties and sprayed some perfume on as well.

"Good girl Yvette. Now, look me in the eyes and tell me if you'll do these things."

I looked into her beautiful, blue, wild eyes while she stroked me through my panties.

"Tell me you will do whatever I ask whenever I ask and not whine about it. Tell me you want to dress and act as much like a woman as you can even if you keep your pee pee."

"I will do anything you ask and I will feminize myself as much as I can even though I don't want to lose my pee pee. Ha ha ha."

"You will be my girlfriend and we will go out together so you can act like a woman and make men crazy and watch me get fucked by real men."

I felt myself get rock hard and Jenna felt it too. "I will be your girlfriend and we will go out so I can act like a woman and make men crazy and watch you get fucked by real men."

Jenna took her hand off of me and gave me a rubber to put on. I put it on. "Stroke yourself. The rubber is for you to come in not for you to fuck me. You already know you can't do a decent job of that right?"

"Right, I'd just come instantly and you and I would feel cheated."

"Good girl Yvette. Now tell me you want to suck a real cock and get fucked in the ass while you watch me fuck."

"Uh, I uh, Oh God sorry Jenna. Wait a second." I had to stop stroking as I thought about what I was going to say since I was ready to come. I waited while it subsided.

Jenna smiled widely at me. "See, that excites you! Stop denying your inner self. You're a woman with a cock. The most valuable kind! Come on girlfriend!"

I came instantly and powerfully. It felt like my whole body came in the tension and release I felt just then. "Ungh! Ungh! GOD! Yes!! Ungh." I came and counted at least twelve spasms. When it was over Jenna took the rubber off and spilled it on the dildo and made me eat it.

"Tastey isn't it sweetie?"

"Uh, yea," I said as I tried to catch my breath. I felt silly in the clothes I had on now and I knew what Jenna's next question was going to be.

"So, now answer me. You came as soon as I said it so tell me the truth, tell me you want to suck a real cock and get fucked. Personally, I want you to. I think you'd love it and it would make me so hot watching." She looked at me waiting.

"Uh, I uh, Jenna, I feel silly in these clothes now and after that come, sucking a cock and getting fucked is the last thing I want to do. Sorry."

Jenna looked at me obviously not pleased. She thought about what to do. "Okay baby, that's okay I guess. You're just denying your true self that's all. I guess you need more time. We can start back to the way it was before with you dressing under your clothes at work and you filling the thermos. On weekends we can start going out more with you dressed as a woman so you can get more used to it and know that that is what you were meant to be. How's that? Like the idea of coming whenever you want again?"

I was surprised. I thought for sure the cage was going back on. This was a real relief. I looked at her as she lay on the pillow next to me. "Thanks sweetie, yea, that would be nice. Let's do that. But do I have to go out dressed like a woman?"

"Yvette, and I will only call you Yvette so you can further get into the role until your ego gives up it's attachment to the past. Yes, Yvette, you will have to be a man, face your fear and go out dressed like a woman. That is the only way you can put aside your old paradigm of yourself. You need to interact with others as a woman. The acceptance and compliments you will get will help to shape your new ego and dissolve your old one so you can be what you are meant to be. If, after some time of doing this you still feel you're not into this, then we can talk about it. Okay? Just promise me to be feminine and pretty and sexy as often as you can and to come as much as possible and enjoy your gifts at doing that. Okay sweetie? I want you to be as happy as you can be."

I kissed Jenna, she smiled and turned off the light as she rolled toward me, snuggled me and we fell asleep.

Two Girls Out for Fun

Jenna had me back into the routine where I was jerking off around 16 times everyday at work. I didn't get much work done anymore but I did fill the thermos every day. We'd go out to dinner or eat in and then go out most nights. Jenna had me dressing up as Yvette whenever we went home.

I was definitely sexually satisfied and had gotten quite good at doing my makeup and choosing outfits to wear. Jenna had been keeping my video supply full of her with the traveling businessmen she took care of each night. I had begun wearing a rubber when we went out since I would come a couple of times from the excitement Jenna would generate when she was seducing the men. Especially with the overflowing come tank of mine that now needed release so often.

"Yvette, are you ready? I think tonight might be the night you suck a cock!" Jenna shouted from the bathroom as she fixed her hair.

"Oh honey, why do you have to keep talking about that!"

"Because I know you'll love it and once you get past the point of fear of that then you'll be ready to take it in another place."

"Jenna please, I'm having a good time as it is," I said as I put the last gold leaf, dangle earring in my ear. I sprayed perfume on my legs, arms and neck. I pulled my suntan stockings up and tightened the straps of the garter to them. I pulled my black satin panties aside and rolled an unlubed, snug fit, condom over my perpetually hard cock and tucked it back in my panties.

I adjusted the bubble hem of the pink flowered minidress and adjusted my gel forms in my bra so my cleavage was maximized. I walked over to the mirror in my five inch heeled, pink satin, strappy, sandals and checked how I looked. Unbelievable! How could I ever think I'm a man! I took a handful of my rubbers from the nightstand and put them in my pink pocketbook and slung it over my shoulder. I walked to the bathroom to Jenna.

"How do I look sweetie!" I stood with one hand on my hip with the long pink nails flashing. Since it was the weekend I didn't have to worry about taking them off so I took the time to put them on tonight.

"Incredible! Yvette, that dress is so flattering for you and your nails came out so nice!" Jenna finished adjusting her gelled hair before it dried. She stood in her six inch heeled, black leather strap sandals, lifted the hem of her short black chiffon dress and adjusted her black stockings garter straps. The corset she wore underneath made her thin waist even thinner and now it must have been no more than twenty inches or so. She leaned over to adjust the ankle bracelet and her nipple jewelry showed as her dressed pulled away. She had gold nooses with little cocks dangling on each nipple keeping them hard.

"Talk about looking awesome! Jenna, you look incredible! I love the nipple jewelry and the six inch heels are enough to make a man come on their own!"

Jenna looked at me and smiled and winked. "I think I'm gonna get laid tonight baby. I've gotten so fucking horny!! Hope you don't mind watching."

What could I say? "Of course not baby. I can't wait." I was excited at the thought though. Terribly excited. Why was I like that? Maybe I did want to be a woman and watching her I, uh, I guess, I really did imagine myself as her when it happened.

Jenna took me by the hand and led me downstairs. She drove the R8 tonight. When we arrived at the club, Jenna found her targets right away. She led us to a table of three of them.

There was a tall black man with wide shoulders and a big bright smile, a blonde haired blue eyed man about like me and then there was a black haired blue eyed man that was almost as large as the black man. They all smiled as we approached the wrap around booth they were in.

"Hello ladies! Like to join us for a few drinks?" The blonde one said as he and the rest of them stood up from the booth and stepped out. "My name is Phil." Her reached out and shook both of our hands. "This is Tony and Bubba." He motioned to each.

Bubba shook my hand first and then Jenna's. I felt like a child in size next to him as his huge hard hand wrapped around mine. Tony was almost as large and hard as well. Tony took my hand and had me get in the booth from the right while Phil got in next from the left to be seated to my right. Phil took Jenna's hand and had her sit next to him. Then Tony got in to my left and Bubba to Jenna's right.

The waiter came over and took our drink orders and returned promptly. We sat and talked while I felt both Phil and Tony's hands on my legs. I crossed them to protect my secret and their caressing of my thighs through the stockings was driving me crazy. I could see that Jenna had Bubba's meat in her hand already from the motion her arm was making beneath the table. Bubba's arm was moving as well, which indicated that he had his fingers inside of Jenna as she sucked his face.

When we were at the point I wasn't going to be able to take it anymore Phil spoke up. "Hey, why don't we go use our private party room upstairs?" Phil pointed above to the curtained rooms on the mezzanine above the dance floor. Tony and Bubba both nodded in agreement as they moved us all from the booth and led us to a curtained off party pit upstairs.

I climbed the stairs with Phil's hand leading me as I looked up and saw Jenna's hand on Bubba's ass and Bubba's huge hand on Jenna's pantied bottom under her dress. Bubba held the red velour curtain aside while we all entered and then closed it on the hook to the side. I could hear the thumping of the music below as we all seated ourselves on the pillowed floor surrounding a large cube coffee table with booze, mixers and snacks on it.

Phil poured drinks for everyone while Jenna fed Bubba olives and rubbed his cock through his pants. Tony was massaging my shoulders.

"What do you think Yvette? Does this party pit look like a good time?" Phil said excitedly.

"It sure does sweetie." I turned and crossed my legs rubbing my knees against his thighs and I rubbed his cock through his pants. Phil put our drinks in front of us on the cube and we both took them and sipped them while we watched Bubba and Jenna.

Jenna now had Bubba's pants undone and she slid them off his huge hard thighs. His cock pressed against the black satin thong he wore straining the fabric. Jenna slid herself between his legs now and slid the thong under his shaved balls. His smooth black cock glistened on the tip with precum as she wrapped both of her tiny hands around the shaft, one atop the other, and then she took as much as she could into her mouth and there was still lots of cock left showing. She stroked and sucked him while he put his huge hand in her hair and held her fast.

Jenna slurped and popped her hot mouth off Bubba's cock and looked at me. She motioned for me to suck Bubba's cock and I shook my head no. Then she motioned her head to Phil and Tony. I looked away from her. She wanted me to suck their cocks and I didn't want to. The old self said no. But, I had to do something for these guys though or they might have raped me.

Jenna was now on all fours and Bubba had her hips in his hands as he shoved that huge cock into her dripping wetness. Jenna's eyes opened wide as he slid in and out of her slowly letting her stretch to take him. I looked at Tony and Phil and thought about what I should do and Phil got up and went to Jenna. He dropped his pants in front of her face and offered his cock to her to suck. Jenna took it appreciatively and now I only had Tony to worry about.

Jenna's moans were muffled by Phil's cock in her mouth as Bubba started to pound her fiercely now. I felt Tony's hand on my leg and I rolled toward him and kissed him on the mouth as I undid his pants with his help. I took a pair of panties out of my purse and wrapped them around his huge cock and started to stroke and squeeze him. I ran my fingernails under his shaved balls and tugged on them while I stroked him faster and faster.

I felt Tony pull me closer with his arm and he kissed me hard now. His cock got rock hard. He pulled away from the kiss and I felt his breath in my ear. "Let me feel your silky hand on me instead of the panties." His warm breath made me tingle. I let go of the panties and wrapped my fingers around his velvety cock. I ran my thumb over the dripping tip and made him twitch. I stroked him as he nearly crushed me to him. I looked over at Jenna.

Phil had come all over Jenna's hard, gelled hair and her face and Bubba now flipped her like a rag doll onto her back. He pushed her legs behind her head and held her pinned down with his hands on the back of her stocking clad thighs just above her knees. Her shoes danced in the air while her feet were pointed with the rigidness of her orgasm as Bubba banged her and she called out to him. "Yes, I'm coming lover! Fuck me with that beautiful cock, fuck me!" If anyone was on the other side of that curtain I'm sure they heard that!

Bubba banged her as he held her riveted to the floor and I could see he was ready to come as Jenna kept coming over and over on his cock. Her body would tense up and shudder each timed she came with her voice moaning with each wave of pleasure. One after the other she came, almost continuously, her body reacted to the huge hard cock as it pressed against her G-spot and filled her up with thrust after thrust after thrust. Her juices were running down his cock and splashing off his balls as he pounded her. Then, he went rigid and cried out a "Ungh" for each time he pushed into her and I saw the come roll out around his cock as he came and Jenna came some more her hands squeezed his hard muscled ass as he did.

Tony had now reached the point of no return and he held me tight as I stroked him and made him come all over my legs and dress. I came simultaneously in my rubber as he did and shuddered in his embrace. We had all come at nearly the same time. I fell against Tony's hard chest as he cradled me and caught his breath then breathed into my ear. "That was one fantastic jerk off babe. I can only imagine what it would be like to get a blow job from you or fuck you!"

Jenna was spent with Bubba's shrinking, but still huge, cock still sliding in and out of her while her eyes were rolled back in her head and she twitched from time to time as her orgasm spent itself through her body. When she settled down she looked at me and saw I hadn't sucked anyone's cock and if her eyes could burn, they would have. She wasn't happy with me.

Bottom Training

I was half asleep dreaming about Tony's cock coming in my hand and the feeling of kissing him. What was happening to me? Here I was getting off on having a man come for me while my wife came on some big black cock. Maybe Jenna was one hundred percent right and I should give up the thought that I'm really a man. I love the feel of women's clothing and the feel of walking in heels. I love putting on makeup and perfume and figuring out outfits from the unlimited choices women have to dress in. I love controlling and making a man crazy with his cock! It was incredible, unbelievable but incredible at the same time! I felt myself come against the sheets as I relived it all seeing it in my mind's eye. It was then that I heard Jenna wake up next to me.

"Morning Jenna."

"Morning Yvette. Today is going to be a little different for you. I see you already came your first time. Probably reliving last night I bet. If that doesn't tell you something nothing will. How will you ever be happy until you get the old self out of you? So, that's why I have a plan. Go to the bathroom and do your toilet, get shaved and showered and use the new attachment on the shower I put in there to clean yourself out. We're off on vacation until I say so."

She kissed me on the cheek as I lay face down on the bed and shook me to get up. I took my shower and shaved everything and cleaned my bottom out with the shower attachment. When I got back to the bedroom the bed was made and Jenna had my clothes picked out on the bed. That horrible cage was there as well. She sat there looking at me. "Yes, the cage is going back on. You need to get used to the thought of sucking a cock and getting laid young lady. Get dressed and make breakfast for us while I shower. And put that cage on! No more coming until I say so."

Jenna took her robe off and walked in her high-heeled slippers and panties to the bathroom. I reluctantly put my cage on wondering how long I would have to wear it now. How stupid can I be?

The clothes Jenna had chosen were pretty slutty yet cute. The bottom of the panties had a hole in them in back with lace sewn around it. Kinda strange.

I slid the stocking up my leg and felt the silkiness of it as it caressed my leg. I attached it in six places to the garter belt and pulled the straps tight so I could feel the pull of the stocking on my feet and against my leg as I moved. I did the other leg enjoying the feeling immensely. I put the panties with the hole in them on. They were black lace and matched the garter belt and bra. I felt the silkiness of the panties brush my bottom and felt my cock swell against the cage it was in trying to grow.

I put the bra on and inserted the gel forms and adjusted my cleavage. A leather mini skirt with an open back side went on next along with a stretch lace, V-neck top. I lifted the skirt and adjusted the V-neck top by tugging at the bottom of it to pull the V-neck down to expose my cleavage. A black leather belt secured it all in place around my waist.

Six-inch fetish high heels in black leather with a studded leather strap around the ankle framed my pretty pink toenails in the open toe style. Black and gold chain earrings went into each of the two holes in each of my ears and a black and gold bandana went around my hair holding it back. I went into the bathroom and did my makeup. As I looked at myself I throbbed in the cage getting hard and ready to come again soon. If I didn't have the damn cage on! When I was done, I sprayed on some perfume, went downstairs and made breakfast while Jenna was getting ready.

Jenna came downstairs. She was dressed in black PVC with a short skirt that had a hole in the front where a cock jutted out, black, PVC, high-heeled boots with a black PVC halter-top and vest. A whip dangled off her belt. She looked very much in charge.

"Nice breakfast Yvette. Thank you. Good thing you decided to make a big breakfast. You'll need all the energy you can get." Jenna seated herself at the table and began eating. After a few bites she spoke again. "Today you'll see that a cock is what you want and that is the way you'll come. And you WILL come only by cock. You will learn that that is what you truly want and that is why you feel so good in women's clothing and look so good in them as well. It is what you are meant to be and today and everyday from now on, you will be learning that until you're sure of who you really are." She smiled, ate another bite of her eggs and crunched on a piece of bacon.

I looked at her not quite sure what to say or do and looked back at my plate of food. I ate it the way she taught me, femininely. I dabbed my lips with my napkin, careful not to wipe off my lipstick and glanced at Jenna quickly. She didn't notice me looking.

"Yes I did, you're not sure what to do. Don't worry baby, trust me, you are going to love this once we kill your old ego. Trust me."

We finished breakfast and Jenna had me clean up while she set things up in the great room. I heard a porn video go in and she backed it up and paused it. I heard her arranging pillows on the floor as she tossed them around the room. When I was done I went in.

Jenna had an arrangement of pillows on the floor with a cock suction cupped to the hardwood floor in the front of a pile of pillows. On the table behind the pillows was a tube of lube and a few vibrators and butt plugs. She stood regally in her outfit with her hand stroking her strap on cock. "Kneel down and let the pillows support you on your chest some. I want you to watch the video and suck the cock on the floor while you do.

Jenna had me make myself comfortable and able to see the video and not get a stiff neck. She then inserted a device in me, which felt like a softer dildo but then she ran cords to a box. First, she attached a belt to the toy that held it fast against my bottom all the way inside of me. She hooked it up and turned it on a little. I could feel a tingling in my bottom now. She looked at me to see my expression and she turned it up a little more. "How's that? Feel nice? See how sensitive that area is? See how good it can feel in there? Now you watch the videos of these shemales getting laid and I'll sit on the couch and watch you enjoy okay?"

I took my mouth off the fake cock I was sucking and bobbing my head on. "Okay Jenna." I went back to sucking it while I watched the videos as these gorgeous women with cocks played with men and sucked their cocks and then, got fucked! My cock was straining against the cage but it wouldn't be able to come this way. At least I didn't think so.

That was until about an hour had passed and Jenna started messing with the toy and then the box it was plugged into. Then she did something that must have inflated it from what I felt. Then she turned on something that made a whirring sound and I could feel it as it stroked inside of me. Finally she made it tingle even more with some sort of electo-stimulator that sent electrical charges through my skin inside making me clench and release. Jenna set a portion of the video on repeat where the girl was sucking a cock and coming on one in her ass and let it loop digitally.

Jenna now lay down on the floor in front of me smiling. "Now you'll see how good things can feel down there. You'll feel as good as the girl on the video. I'm going to take a shower and then we can be done for the day since I think by then you'll need a rest. Go ahead and sit on the couch."

Jenna stood, carried the box and cords and put them behind the couch as I sat down feeling it all going crazy inside of me. I could barely walk to the couch it was so intense. She handed me a coffee mug. "Catch the come in this as it comes through the cage as I'm sure it will." It was already dripping when I sat down. I looked at the girl on the video enjoying herself and then all of a sudden my world changed. Jenna cranked the thing up all the way.

The thing inside of me was pounding me in rhythm with the girl being pounded in the video along with vibrating wildly and electro stimulating me. I felt my cock straining against the cage. It streamed come out of it while I literally stayed at the very peak of an orgasm. I had a hard time breathing it was so intense. Jenna came in front of me and stuck the cock in my mouth. "I turned it all the way up. Enjoy!" I watched the shemale and sucked the cock and felt my body fill with endorphins as I flowed continuously. I didn't come in pulses, I just rode the edge of just before you come squirt. I had that intense feeling but no release with the normal ejaculations that happen. I couldn't move to release my self the pleasure was so great. Yet, I wasn't able to be finished.

Before I knew it, it seemed, Jenna came back. "Well, a whole hour of coming, my my, look at the amount of come you leaked. The whole mug is almost full to spilling! And you didn't even touch your cock, how about that!" She turned it all off at once and I untensed and collapsed into the couch. "Good, now, you can come a week after my period is over. Till then, this is how you will come for ten seconds a day. That is the time it takes a man's cock to ejaculate versus being milked by a cock like you were just now. You will also dress strictly as a man and will not shave your body."

Agreeing to Change

Two weeks later, having worn the cage and being milked only ten seconds a day after being used to coming 16 times a day at work and more at night, I was one horny guy and boy did I want to feel a cock in my ass! Or anything that would make me come. I sipped my coffee as I thought about how those milkings teased me so much and all I could think of is the hour long come I had watching the shemale in the video come with me. At least I thought I wanted a cock in my ass then. My body was itchy and hairy and felt dirty to me since I hadn't shaved it in so long. I was ready to be Yvette once more and would do anything Jenna wanted.

"So, you didn't answer me.

"Uh, okay." I thought about what she said and in my heart I knew that would be exciting. Jenna was a doctor in psychiatry. She knew my inner workings better than I even did, I guessed.

My hand fell to my lap and resumed my stroking Jenna allowed me to do just having taken the cage off me while I was in my dreamland thinking. I readied my statement. "Uh, I want to suck cock and get fucked in the ass and watch you fuck. Oh God! I'm coming!" I came like a rocket that had been over fueled. With all those days of arousal watching Jenna and never once coming but the ten seconds a day she milked me, I came over and over. I felt at least twelve huge jets rush out of my cock into the condom. I twitched and shuddered as I came and then slumped is my chair exhausted. I felt Jenna take the condom off. When she returned she gave me a kiss.

"I love you Yvette! I'll type our agreement up tomorrow morning and since it's Saturday I think we should go shopping and then go out. I'll schedule surgery for Sunday with my colleague. He won't mind doing it then for me and you'll be ready for next weekend with a brand new set of real boob implants. Don't worry, the recovery takes only three days for over the muscle implants and you'll be asleep all of that time. After that they will be a little uncomfortable for a few days but by the weekend you'll be ready to put them to work. I'll have electrolysis done on the few hairs you have on your body while you sleep so you'll never have to shave anything again. Even your pee pee will be smooth as a pickle, well, ha ha ha a gerkin. Ha ha ha."

Now that I came I had a different view on doing this. Boob surgery? I never thought she'd go that far.

Do I Have to Suck One?

It was Saturday morning and Jenna had picked out a denim mini skirt for me, a pink tight blouse with a V-neck, suntan thigh highs, four inch strappy denim heels, pink bra and panties and there were a set of silicone breasts on the bed.

"Yup, I got those some time ago knowing you would reach this stage. You'll get a sampling of what it will be like to have boobs by wearing them. They won't feel as nice as the real ones will but it will give you an idea of the weight and bounce. Now shower, shave your disgusting body, and get dressed and I'll have breakfast ready for you. You can wear my pink dangle earrings and necklace and you can do your makeup and toenails. Leave the fingers alone and we'll get them done at the spa along with your hair." Jenna left the room and went downstairs before I could say anything. I did as I was told.

It felt great to get the hair that had grown on my legs and chest and so on off my body so I could feel the fabrics, nice and silky against it now. It actually felt great to be dressed this way and I managed to do pretty well with my makeup and hair. The perfume was refreshing to be able to wear again and I was feeling that I had made a good decision once more as I relished in the sensations. I looked in the mirror and felt every bit like an Yvette as my free cock rubbed the panties I wore.

Jenna had made a wonderful poached egg breakfast and fresh squeezed orange juice for me. She had a list of the things we were to do today, that I only caught a glimpse of, as well as a document for me to sign.

As I ate she sucked my cock and allowed me to read the document while she did. She brought me to the edge several times and I took my time eating and enjoying the attention she was giving me. I signed the page on both lines, the line with my old legal name and the one with my new legal name. Attached was a document for the lawyer to change my name to Yvette. I signed that as well. Also attached was the request for breast augmentation that was signed by my doctor wife and I signed as well. My fear in signing the documents was overcome by the sensations of Jenna sucking me and the feeling of coming soon. I was about to come as I felt Jenna flick her tongue over my hole. I finished signing all of them and Jenna gave a good stroke with her lips and as she felt me come she put a glass in front of my cock as she stroked it. She stood, put the glass on the table, snatched up the papers and smiled.

"Good job Yvette, everything will be wonderful for us both very soon. Drink this." She handed me the glass with the come. I poured it into my coffee and stirred it in. "Now I'll get ready while you clean up down here and have your coffee and then we can accomplish the list."

Jenna came down dressed in similar fashion to me and I was feeling a bit of trepidation. "Jenna, you realize I've never gone out in public during the day dressed as Yvette. I'm a little nervous."

"Oh hush!" Jenna said as she came and knelt before me as I sat in the kitchen chair. She ran her hands over my stockinged legs and looked me in the eye with her beautifully done makeup. "Honey, your makeup is flawless, your hair beautiful, your walk perfect, what else could there be to give you away."

"My voice?"

"Heck no. Your voice is more like a woman's than a man's. If you want, try to talk from your head instead of your chest and it will raise it up a little."

"Like this?"

Yes, try saying something more. Like how you love being Yvette and how you can't wait to suck a cock."

"Uh, I can't wait to suck a cock and I love being Yvette."

"Perfect. Let's go and stop worrying. You drive since you need to learn how to drive in a skirt and heels."

We took Deebee out and fired her twelve cylinders up going down the back roads. It felt incredible with these clothes on. Once more my senses were heightened and I felt totally alive. Jenna caressed my right thigh while I drove and before I knew it we were there.

"Okay, a new haircut for Yvette and some nice long salon nails."

"How will I go to work with new nails and haircut?"

"Work? C'mon girl. I forgot to tell you. I've given you a to die for retirement package and you couldn't refuse!"

"Retire at the age of thirty six?"

"Well, not retire but you'll have plenty to do as Yvette once you're fully into the role. You wouldn't want to work a real job then. Trust me."

"Well, I guess that takes the pressure off of worrying about what I would do at work. I wasn't getting much done lately anyway, coming every half an hour. Let's go all out then."

"That's the spirit girl!" Jenna kissed me on the cheek and we continued walking through the mall to the spa. I could feel my new breast forms as they moved ever so slightly and I could feel them tug on my chest pulling the bra straps with each step. Walking in heels was second nature to me now and it actually felt better than walking in my flat-heeled men's shoes. I loved the click of our heels as we made our way. We got lustful looks from each guy we passed no matter what the age. I couldn't see anyone thinking I wasn't what I presented. We arrived at the spa.

Jenna checked us in at the desk. "Yvette is here for her cut, highlight and manicure."

"Thanks," said the receptionist. "It will be about fifteen minutes.

"Thanks!" Jenna said as we both sat on the couch. Jenna picked up a few of the haircut style magazines and we both perused them. She saw one that was perfect for my length of hair, face shape and message it sent. "Oh Yvette, this is it. It cries out your name! It's the same length so you wouldn't lose much. It has beautiful highlights that accent the textured shaggy shape and it cries out sexy and hot to trot! What do you think?"

I took the book from her and tried to imagine the style on myself and the more I looked at it the more I liked it. I stood and looked in the mirror holding the magazine up next to my face. Perfect. Talk about a sexy hot blonde! I looked at Jenna and smiled ear to ear. "Yes! This is incredible. You think it will look like that on me when it's done?"

"Don't worry, the girl doing you is the best. She'll get it perfect."

I turned and looked in the mirror again and tussled my hair. I adjusted its fall on my shoulders. I felt I had to reapply my lipstick for some reason. I took it out of my purse and did it, then sprayed a light spritz of perfume on each wrist so I could smell it. I looked back at Jenna.

"Yvette, you are such a girlie girl. Can't pass a mirror without fixing something. I love you baby. See, this is gonna be great!" Jenna winked and laughed.

"Yvette?" Came the call from the haircutter and the manicurist. They took me back as I excitedly asked about the cut and she agreed it was perfect for me and would come out great. They seated me and started right in. One washed my hair while the other started on my nails buffing them and cleaning up the cuticles. She sat me up and showed me the colors she would highlight with and started with that while the other applied the nails and nail color.

When the girl was finished with my nails I couldn't stop feeling them and letting my fingertips feel how smooth they were. I watched in the mirror as my new look fell into place. Lastly, the cutter asked if she could shape my eyebrows a bit and I agreed. She thinned them to a high arching line and brushed them in with a color pencil and brush, which she then handed to me to keep.

"Thank you! I feel incredible! I feel like a new me. You did such a wonderful job!" I said using my newer, higher, voice, which seemed to come quite naturally.

"You're welcome. Enjoy the rest of your day you beautiful thing!"

I paid with Jessie's credit card thinking that would have to change at some point. When I hesitated, Jenna noticed. "Don't worry that will be taken care of by the lawyer along with your drivers license and so on. You signed the papers today remember?" I looked at Jenna and smiled but felt a pang of uncertainty at the thought of changing my name. She took my arm and led us out.

"How does it all feel? The hair and the nails?"

I ran my hand through my new hair and it felt awesome. I stopped thinking about the name change and thought about what Jenna asked me. "Not tangly like my old hair. It's silky and has movement when I walk. The nails feel incredible," I said truthfully as I held them out for Jenna to see, long talons with square tips. "I think it might take some getting used to with the nails but I did manage to get my credit card out and that's the most important thing. The cut was highlighted beautifully and I love the way it fits my face and feels when I walk. You've given me more sensations to revel in. Thanks Jenna!"

"No, thank you for finding yourself. You had the courage to do this not me."

"I wouldn't have done it without you though. I'm too much of a wimp for that. No balls ya know!" We both laughed as we moved on with our shopping. For both of us we bought shoes, necklaces, earrings, watches and bracelets, blouses and tops, skirts and dresses, and lots of stockings, garter belts, bras and panties of every variety. I wasn't sure where we would put it all when we got home but we had it all.

We took a break for lunch leaving our things at the security center for delivery to the house when we said to. When you shop like this they take good care of you. They even take all the tags off for you and give you hangers and all, repacking it for ease of putting away. No boxes and things to deal with after.

Lunch was at a café outside the mall, in the shade, with a beautiful, warm breeze that blew across my legs and up my skirt. We ate raw oysters and clams with crisp crackers and a very light white wine.

69

"How about our waiter Yvette? I think he's interested in you."

"No way. Stop Jenna. I can't do that. Not yet please. Don't rush me."

"I'm sorry Yvette. I thought I saw you cross your legs in response to him as if he stirred you down there. My mistake."

"Uh, well, maybe I did but I have to grow the balls first okay? 'Balls!,' said the queen, 'if I had two I'd be king! Not because I want two, but because I'd have to!'"

"Yes dear, for sure you will not be king. Don't worry, your girlfriend will make it easy for you to enjoy your new self." Jenna put her hand on mine as the waiter came back and dropped the bill. He smiled and winked at me with his white teeth and left. I paid the bill with cash and left him a nice tip with a spray of perfume on the bill. Now that's a good idea, he'll smell that bill all day! One more stop and we'll go home and take a nap so you're rested for tonight"

Jenna had me drive to a seedier part of town where there was an adult book/video/adult toy store. We both went in and Jenna grabbed two baskets and handed one to me. She went up and down the aisles and grabbed things and put them in the baskets. Vibrators for cocks, vibrators for holes, butt plugs and butt plugs with vibrators. Condoms of all sorts and flavors even. Nipple clamps and cock straps, and on and on. Even an enema bag and a chastity device for men, that professed to be the most comfortable and sensual one in existence. It had a straighter shape that didn't restrict as much and was lined in satin with a gel filling. It had a place to put a vibrator or to hang jewelry on it as it had a piece of jewelry and vibrator in the package showing the way they went on. Jenna took another look around the store grabbing some lubes and crotchless panties. Then she hit the video section and selected some of those shemale videos and big cock gangbang videos. She went to the counter with all of our stuff.

"Hi, we're having a party. It's not all for us," Jenna said as she smiled at him. He was big and handsome with blond hair, blue eyes, rippling biceps and a bulge in his pants.

"A party? Can I come AT it?" He looked at both of us as he said that and then his eyes locked on mine as he winked. I felt my heart almost stop, as I got nervous.

Jenna spoke for me. "Yea, if the party is now, I can tell that Yvette has a desire to look at you a little closer."

I felt my face blush and I looked at Jenna with fright on my face. The guy behind the counter looked around and whispered to Jenna just loud enough for me to hear it too. "We can go in back. I'm pretty quick when I want to be and trust me I could use the favor today. You think Yvette is willing? I'm not getting that vibe from her."

Jenna looked at me with a look of, "You better straighten up and have balls." I looked back at him and he looked like a puppy begging for a treat. He smiled at me as he waited.

"Sorry, just a little nervous today, too much coffee. I'd love to see what's under your hood and maybe try one of those cherry flavored things on it." I smiled and hoped my shaking voice didn't give away my trepidation. He looked around again, came out from behind the counter and yelled to a guy across the store stocking shelves to cover the register since he had a call he had to take in the back.

He led us to a back room littered with porn magazines and cleared a spot on the desk for him to sit. He threw a pillow on the floor for me to kneel on. Jenna took my purse and handed me a cherry rubber, magnum sized. I knelt on the floor.

My hands were shaking as I struggled with my new nails to open the package. He took the package from me.

"Let me help little lady."

I looked up at his huge body. "I just got these nails and I haven't gotten used to them yet. Sorry." I reached for his zipper, pulled it down and he undid his pants and dropped them and his underwear to the floor.

He was totally shaved down there, thank God, and his dick was semi hard as I wrapped my hand around the base. I stroked him as I looked at it taking it all in while my heart raced in my throat. I had never seen a big cock like that up close and certainly never saw a cock from this angle. I was used to seeing mine below me. This was something else entirely. He handed me the rubber.

"Thanks," I squeaked out of my tightened nervous vocal cords. I looked at Jenna as she was rubbed herself through her skirt while she watched me. I was so happy knowing she enjoyed watching ME now. I looked back and rolled the rubber over his thick shaft. It stretched far and rolled slowly since he was probably a magnum plus size or something. I looked at it as I got it all on the monster and stroked him. I was lost in wonderment looking at it. I relaxed a little now as I got more involved and engaged in what I was doing and my heart slowed noticeably as my cock swelled beneath my skirt. I felt the thickness and the hardness of his cock and marveled at how big a man's cock can be. No wonder I can't do much for Jenna. This is what they're supposed to be like. My cockette throbbed. Then I heard him.

"That's good baby, now let's have those teeth run down that rubber and heat me up. With a rubber on you can be pretty rough and it's okay." I took him in my mouth smelling and tasting the cherry flavor and pushed my tongue firmly into his hole through the rubber. I slipped it back and forth, with his precum lubricating it inside, and made him twitch. He grabbed my head and twisted my hair in his hand for a good grip. I rubbed my crotch through my skirt with my left hand and stroked his cock with my right while I sucked it. I was so excited. I shouldn't have been, a guy being excited about sucking a cock, but I went with the feeling and couldn't help being as excited as if I landed on the moon. I wasn't really feeling like a guy anyway.

My eyes closed, he started to pump into my face and I had to put both hands on it now to keep him from choking me as I smelled his cologne and the cherry rubber. "Look up at me baby," he said and I did. I could see his face contort as he all out fucked my face and I tightened my grip on his meat. I heard him grunt and tense up as he looked me in the eyes and then I felt his come as his rod swelled in my hand with each release. I felt the come as it pumped under my fingers, through his cock and jettisoned into the rubber and my mouth. I felt it slide over his cock while he continued to pound me. I kept my eyes locked on his but I blinked my eyes uncontrollably as he came. Then he stopped and just held me there. I rolled my eyes to the left and saw that Jenna had come and was straightening her skirt. I looked up at him and he still held me tight. He stroked my hair and I felt him going limp in my mouth.

He started to pump though my fist and into my mouth again slowly and I felt him get harder again. He was going to do it again! I held his cock with both hands so he could feel the constriction on all of its length. The come made it slick inside the rubber as I stroked him. I flicked my tongue over the head and bit it gently now and he responded by quickening his pace. I did it some more and pulled on his ball sack with my other hand. He cried out. "Oh baby! Yea! You know how to suck a cock. Ungh!" He squeezed my head so tight now it felt as if he'd crush it. He was rock hard once more.

He fucked my face and came again. I felt it rush in his cock under my fingers, past my tongue at the tip and then it leaked past my hand and down his cock getting onto my hands. He slowed again and held me still while he stroked gently and moaned quietly. I felt him going soft again and wondered if he was going to do it again. He stroked and stroked through my hands clenched around his meat and into my mouth going gently and enjoying the sensations as his come dripped over my hands and fell on my skirt.

He stopped and pulled out leaving the rubber in my hands as I came in my panties and felt what felt like a pop bottle full of come squirt through the panty fabric and wet my skirt. It didn't stop there but continued to go down my thigh, dripped on the floor and on my ankles. I wiped it off the stockings on my ankle and licked my fingers so as not to waste it as

73

Jenna always said. I stood and felt it sticky against my thick skirt and looked down to see that it didn't show. My face felt hot from blushing and I smiled, a now reluctant and embarrassed smile, at him knowing I had never come so hard and so much in my life, without electronics that is.

"Oh baby, you are good! I almost thought I'd get a third but, oh well, no such luck." He lifted his pants, turned around snatched the rubber from my hand and threw it into the trash where several others were. He pulled his pants up, tucked himself in and zipped up. "Let's get you girls checked out."

He went to the counter and rang up one basket and then packed it. He packed the second basket without ringing it. "This one's for the favor you did for me today gorgeous. I haven't felt that good in a long time. Maybe we can get together sometime huh?"

"Yea, uh, maybe we can," I said and took the one bag and Jenna took the other. "My name is Yvette. Thanks for your donations, all of them!" Jenna and I walked out with our haul.

"Nice job Yvette. See how much you pleased him? That's the way all the guys will feel. Remember, your hot and in control. They will do anything to get their rocks off with you. Was it fun? I came just watching you."

"It was quite an unexpected experience."

"Yea, but was it fun?"

"Ugh, definitely an understatement. Shocking maybe, overwhelming, exciting as hell."

Caged Again

Jenna and I went home and I was somewhat listless and spent. I told her it was just a bit overwhelming for me and we watched an old 50's movie while I cuddled with her on the couch. I held her arm in my hands and put my head on her shoulder thinking she maybe was right because I did it and I enjoyed it immensely when I was doing it. Maybe this was what I was. After I came though, I felt all the remorse. I thought that I was just fucked up and I shouldn't be this way. I felt like a freak.

We ate an early supper, watched another movie and went to sleep early. Jenna put out a pretty new outfit for me to wear that felt absolutely luscious on. It was a satin and chiffon nightgown with panties with a sheath in them for my maleness. The sheer silky sheath held it in sensual heaven as the outfit did me. I slid under the satin sheets Jenna had scented with my favorite perfume and fell into a deep but fit full sleep with dreams that I wished I didn't have.

I woke to Jenna whispering in my ear while I came through the sheath, in her hand, in the fabric of my nightgown. "That's it baby, imagine sucking cock like you did yesterday and feel how good it felt."

I came violently once more, as much and as hard, as I did in the store then felt spent and embarrassed once more. I rolled over onto my side and cuddled Jenna with tears dripping from my eyes.

"What's wrong princess? Why are you crying?"

"I'm not crying."

"Then why is my shoulder wet where your head lies? What's the matter?"

"I feel like a freak. I'm not a princess! I'm a man and I shouldn't be having these feelings."

"You're the farthest thing from a man I know! No offense sweetie but it's true. You know how well you've come lately! How about how much and how hard you came sucking that cock. And how hard and well you came just now? You WANT to do what you're doing. It's titillating and exciting and incredibly sensual to you. You are just fighting your desires based on some paradigms you have. Don't you think?"

"You mean, I'm fighting with my inner self due to my preconceived notions of what I am?"

"Exactly! Think if we never answered our desires where we would be? Think about if I followed my parent's conception of me being a housewife and marrying some hunky guy with money. How happy do you think I'd be? I might like to fuck him but what else would I have? We wouldn't be together and I wouldn't be able to love you. I wouldn't be a successful and powerful woman. Think about if you never followed your desire to be a software programmer when your dad wanted you to be a tough manufacturing guy and run his business after he left. How much would you have enjoyed that if you hadn't followed your desires and only fought them and acquiesced to his wishes? These are all paradigms that we broke to get to where you are today."

"Uh, I guess."

"And think about the way you busted through the accepted practice of software patterning and development to achieve your programs that set the world afire. You violated all the standard practices even as your piers and boss were telling you not to. That's what made you the best software developer in the country and earned you your stellar salary. Think about if you hadn't done so. You're a rebel by nature, why is this so hard baby?"

Jenna ran her hand through my hair and kissed me on my lips. She wiped the remaining tears from the corners of my eyes. I stared into her eyes and felt her sincerity. "I love you Jenna. I guess you're right. It's just another paradigm though this one is probably just more ingrained in my belief system of my identity than the others. This is a core issue having to deal with who and what I really am and I guess I've defined myself inaccurately compared to what I really am. Is that it? Is it that simple? If so, what am I, and is it okay to feel like I do? Is it okay to want the things I want and to want what I want for you? Will we survive the changes?"

Jenna stood me up from the bed and arranged my nightclothes around me. She brushed my now silky and shapely hair as she stood me before the mirror and I watched her. "Look at yourself and tell me that what you want is incongruous with who stands before the mirror. You are gorgeous as a woman and soon will be even more gorgeous and yet, you will have the parts of a man as well.

What is wrong with your desires? Will they hurt you or anyone else? Are they against what we want for us? Will they affect our financial position or make us poor? I think not. What then could be wrong other than your beliefs being out of line with reality? A very common thing for many people." Jenna kissed me on the cheek.

"You can't get like this every time you come or I just won't let you come okay?" She smiled and kissed me on the lips and then pinched my ass and squeezed my ass cheeks in her hand pulling me toward her. She rubbed her thigh into my crotch. "So, if you want to cancel our plans I'll rip up the papers. They're really meaningless anyway. They're just a way to get you to commit mentally. If they didn't help, they are meaningless. It's up to you sweetie. Take your time." Jenna took the cage out of the drawer and helped me put it on then she locked it in place.

Tortured to Need

The week went by with Jessie and I together all day every day. She decided to work from home so I wouldn't be alone. I didn't feel right going into the office since I didn't think I could part with my new feminine being. I suppose I could of if I wasn't looking like I am now, but I was now retired anyway. Jessie made sure I was dressed pretty and sexy all week and she kept me on the edge once more by sucking my cock, masturbating in front of me while I had my cock cage on so I couldn't come, and generally getting me to such a point of libido and arousal that I was literally feeling like a cat in heat. She wouldn't let me come though. By then, I wanted nothing more than to have a man and have my wife have a real man. I wouldn't admit it to Jenna though, even though I had admitted it to myself. The weekend came around and it was Friday at lunch when Jenna gave me our agenda for the weekend.

"Yvette, honey. I think we should take it easy this weekend and go to a mountain cottage what do you think, some time alone in the woods and hills? I made a reservation in the hills of New York where there are great restaurants and nightclubs if we want to go out or we could just stay and be served by the resident staff in the mountain home. What do you think?"

Jenna came over to me on the couch and sat next to me. She crossed her stockinged legs over mine as she adjusted the pinstriped suit skirt and coat. She sat revealing her luscious thirty-two C's pushed up in her lace bra. They showed from the low button placement of the satin

79

blouse. The blouse matched the pinstripes of her power suit. She always dressed this way when she worked, even when she stayed home to work. Her five inch heeled black pump now dangled off one of her feet as she bounced her leg.

"It's the Fourth of July holiday and that sounds like just the thing to settle me down."

"Yes, a break is good. Your libido has been building up nicely with the cage and teasing I've been giving you. I'll let you come at some point when we're there. I picked up a new trial prescription for you as well that will allow you to retain the libido without having to do the feast and famine technique we've been using so if you take them for me you can choose when you come on your own, okay?" Jenna ran her hand through my hair and brushed it back from my forehead. She adjusted the lapels on the work suit I was wearing that she had me wear when we were both working at home.

I leaned back to see Jenna's face better and grinned. "Do you really think I'll need a libido enhancer when I had been coming 16 times a day and then milking me for only ten seconds a day, and then the cage and teasing for the last week with no coming? Won't that be a little overkill? "

Jenna smiled a Cheshire cat grin. "Not overkill, just enhancement. I want you to feel all of your desires to their maximum so you can determine what your true nature is. The feelings you have after you come are NOT you."

"Is it really my true nature when it's enhanced or I'm tortured into that state?"

Jenna swung her legs off me, stood and straightened her skirt and coat. She adjusted the long pointed tendril sideburn by her ear. She felt the tendrils that draped over her collar running her fingers through them to space them out evenly. Her jet-black hair was black as coal with the gel in it and the texture was thick, hard and intense looking. "Does it feel good and do you enjoy it? Does it harm you or anyone else? Or, is it just something that you think shouldn't be the way for a person to be? These are the answers we're looking for, are they not?"

Her blue blue eyes looked blinklessly into mine now as I sat looking up at her from the leather couch. I felt the smooth silkiness of my legs as they crossed and my hands rested themselves with their long fingernails in my lap as my little cock throbbed under them in its cage. I felt as if I was outside this body feeling it. "I guess you're right. That is the objective. Why not!?" I stood and gave her a hug and a kiss. "Thanks for helping me honey."

"Anytime my sweet Yvette! Let's clean up and shut the place up for our trip. I've packed all your things and hung a nice summer dress in your closet, on the near end, along with all the accessories and things for the drive.

Deloto and Newgen

Girls on Vacation

I finished loading Deebee for the ride. Jenna wanted me to drive since she said she had some final correspondence she wanted to get done on the 4G while we drove.

Jenna had picked out a beige summer dress that stopped about six inches below my crotch. It had white gardenias and white and pink orchids in the pattern. She had a gardenia for me to wear in my new haircut behind one ear and gardenia perfume. I felt like a flower myself when I was dressed in the sheer silky thigh highs, white flowered panties with a slip sheath and pouch for my maleness, (NO CAGE!!! I thought I'd come just putting them on!) I had a white flowered 34C bra with gel forms that pushed up my cleavage. They felt firm and full as the bra hugged my chest and I felt the straps pull on my shoulder from their weight.

The shoes matched the dress perfectly and their five-inch heels made my walk sway and bounce seductively. The dangling earrings in my pierced ears had feathers the colors of the flowers in my dress and fluttered against my neck as I moved. A matching necklace sat resting in my cleavage. A short denim, crop top, vest topped off the outfit with a gardenia tucked into the buttonhole, which added scent and beauty to the soft cotton.

I marched myself back upstairs to grab the last things for the trip. My orchid print purse with lipstick, blush, perfume and smokes and two unsweetened iced teas from the fridge. Jenna was ready with her purse and laptop as she looked around the kitchen. "Ready sweetie? How do those new panties feel? I had them made special for you and have matching bras for all of them." Jenna ran her hand under my dress and rubbed me there. "Mmm, nice, I see you like them since you're nice and hard right now. That should make it easy for you to stay alert driving while I finish the last arrangements for the trip on my laptop. Everything ready to go?"

"Deebee is all packed and ready. I have the address loaded into the GPS and we're ready to go."

Jenna adjusted the outfit she wore. It was like mine but with a black background instead of beige and she had a black denim crop vest instead of the blue one like mine. She looked gorgeous as usual. She wrapped her arms around my waist and leaned back looking at me with those intense eyes. "I can't wait, you're going to love this week off. I promise!" She looked at the watch on her wrist. "We should be there before supper time. Let's go. Oh, here, take the first of your pills." Jenna opened her purse and opened a prescription bottle. She shook out a small pink pill for me. She put it on my tongue. "They have a candy coating so you can just swallow it. The dose is three per day, one at each meal."

I swallowed it and we were off on our vacation.

Jenna opened the door on Deebee for me and I sat on the edge of the seat, slipped my hands under my dress and rotated into the bucket seat. She closed the door, came around to the passenger side and got in. Deebee's leather seats felt cool and slick beneath my barely clad bottom. Her twelve cylinders and five hundred horsepower effortlessly purred after I touched the start button. The garage door went up simultaneously from Jenna's long nailed finger pushing the button on Deebee's roof line.

We backed out and the GPS started to talk in the woman's British accent as it found the satellites and calculated the time of arrival. Jenna was already typing on the laptop sending e-mails or IM's, I couldn't tell since she had a privacy screen only visible from head on. She did this for about half an hour with giggles and "Oh yeas!" Occasionally she'd run her hand over my thigh and say what a good week this was going to be. I had no clue what she was up to.

"What are you so busy at there Jenna?" I had to ask.

Deebee's engine purred deeply as we sped down the freeway enroute to our get away. Jenna looked at me smiling and not quite knowing what to say. Then she looked out her window away from me and responded. "Just making arrangements for people to take care of us. You know, someone to cook for us and clean and so on." She looked back now. Somehow I felt that wasn't the real story or at least all of it since she couldn't look at me when she said it. But I wasn't going to push it anymore.

As I thought about this unusual vacation, being constantly dressed as a woman, , my body felt somewhat strange as we drove on. It seemed as if my skin and senses had become heightened. My whole seat and crotch area seemed to tingle with pleasure and my legs felt as if someone were caressing them the way the stockings felt on them. My breasts felt as if they had become real and I could swear I felt my nipples against the fabric of the bra. I looked at my arm as my long, pink, fingernailed hand held the steering wheel and I expected to see something enveloping the skin of my arm, caressing it. My fingertips were alive with sensation and the burled wood of the steering wheel seemed to have an energy all it's own that I felt through my fingers and palms. I rubbed my arm and it felt as if I could make my hand come.

Jenna ran her hand over my thigh and I almost twitched from the feel of it. She looked at me as I drove. "Feels nice huh? The pills are working."

"Is that what this is? It feels incredible! Am I going to feel like this all the time when I take them or does this wear off?"

"It wears off slightly. You're feeling the first time. But it will still be fairly intense. After taking them for a day you can take two or more when you want to experience what you're feeling now. You can't overdose on these. They are perfectly safe. No other side effects either. Quite the drug don't you think? They're all natural as well. A special secret recipe found in some scrolls. They were used for a king's concubines and wives."

"Wow, lucky girls. Have you tried them?"

"Are you kidding? I've been taking them for weeks already. I wanted to be sure they were safe before I gave them to you." Jenna ran her hands over her breasts and down her legs caressing herself all over. "Mmm, See?" She looked forward as we approached the mountain regions. "See up there? See the bald spot at the top of the mountain? That's the clearing for the backyard at the place we are staying. The mansion itself is in the woods shaded by the trees."

"Mansion? I thought we were going to a cabin."

"Well, it kinda is a cabin being in the woods and all, but a really big one. Ha ha ha!"

We drove for another half an hour and lost sight of the top of the mountain. We snaked Deebee through the winding roads and climbed to the top of the mountain. I felt my high-heeled shoes as I moved them from pedal to pedal pushing Deebee faster and harder around each corner. The feel of driving in the high heels was as exciting as the drive was. I felt as if I were a part of Deebee as she quietly growled with each acceleration coming out of each turn. She'd press me back into her seat. The wings of the seat held me firmly as we took gee's in the turns while Bach surrounded us. I felt my cock hard and excited against the fabric of the specially made, and oh so sensual panties.

All of a sudden we were at the gates of the mansion. They swung open for us and I drove the last mile up to it. I pulled around the fountain in front of the stone steps on the marble cobblestones. I turned off Deebee and let out a deep sigh.

Jenna laughed. "Quite the ride wasn't it. Don't worry, we can rest on the patio now and have something to drink."

A man in a butlers suit approached the car and opened Jenna's door helping her out. "Don't worry about your bags or the car. I will take care of them all. Please go inside and the maid will show you around." He then came to my side and helped me out of the car. His big hand grabbed mine securely and his soft callous less flesh spoke of a man who did little

86

hard labor. He was about six foot four and as handsome as a special agent in a spy movie.

Jenna led the way up the marble stairs to the tall, griffin carved, double door entrance. The door opened with a man in black hot-pants shorts, with a ruffled maids bib tied around his neck and attached to his shorts. He was about five foot eight and shaped like a triangle with wide shoulders, narrow hips and a large bulge in his shorts, which put mine to shame. "My name is Roster since I keep track of the people passing through. Please, follow me and I'll show you around."

He turned and walked before us as his firm and round ass cheeks peeked from the bottoms of his shorts. His powerful legs strode barefoot up the velvet carpeted curved staircase to the next floor. He walked and waved his arm as we passed the different rooms. "Study, library, music room." He walked into the next room. "Your dressing rooms." He waved his arms at the room with the makeup tables and dressing divans. He went through an arched doorway where there was a closet with a good thirty feet of various clothing hung in both of our sizes. He walked past them and ran his hand over them which made them flow in his wake.

Below the clothes were high heels all at least five inches high or more. There were dressers in the expanse of wall as well, that he opened the drawers of to reveal bras and panties, garter belts and stockings, corsets and other undergarments. The dressers had jewelry in velvet holders for earrings and necklaces, bracelets and anklets. The one thing I noticed was there were no pants, and no long dresses, except for gowns with rising front hems, and there was no sort of casual clothing I could see except for what looked like a pair of jeans and a shirt on a shelf above the clothes.

He went through the archway at the end and entered into a huge room. "Your bedroom." He motioned for us to enter with his arm and Jenna and I walked in. The ceiling was about twenty feet high with a domed ceiling a good fifty feet in diameter that had windows around the vertical sides of it letting in the natural light.

The dome itself was made up of gilded sections, each framing a lustful scene of a man and a woman or, two women or, two men or, multiple partners together in embraces. In all of the scenes the participants were highly aroused with hard cocks and nipples on bodies of perfect proportions. They were either penetrating, being penetrated, performing fellatio, being fondled or, otherwise in a state of ecstasy. The paintings looked like they were done a century ago but were still perfect. I felt my jaw hanging open in awe as I stared up. I had to ask. "Roster___?"

"Yes, one hundred and twenty seven years old. Painted right here. Restored two years ago in preparation for your arrival." He smiled and moved around the room pointing out things. "The fire will light by pressing this button. It has been converted to gas for your convenience. The temperature control for the room is here." He put his hand behind a red velvet curtain. "The bath is there." He pointed to a switch back entrance, no door.

The bed was beneath a posted bed cover with mirrors beneath facing down on the bed. The bed itself was at least as large as a double king size bed but in the shape of a heart and the posts were all carved with naked bodies of men and women. The carvings were of men with hard cocks and women with hard nipples and shapely bodies. There was even one with both a cock and breasts and the body shape of a woman. As I approached it, the face looked astoundingly like mine and the cock was embarrassingly the same as mine. I gasped when I saw it. "Oh my god!"

Roster responded, "I must say it is a very good likeness. Quite flattering Miss Yvette. Now I will take my leave and let you freshen up. Dinner will be served downstairs. Why not go onto the patio for a drink before dinner. We'll be eating in about an hour." Roster walked out of the room and left through the bedroom door rather than through the dressing room. His bare feet padded softly when he transitioned from the velvet carpet to the marble tile.

I looked at Jenna and I could see she saw my look of awe and surprise. She laughed lightly and stood in front of me with her arms around my neck. She kissed me on the lips with her tongue and I felt that wild tingle throughout my body. She reached down and caressed my cock through my dress. "How are you feeling baby? A little overwhelming isn't it. You'll see though, it will feel like home quickly."

Jenna knelt down and took my cock out of the pouch in my panties and slurped it between her lips making me shudder. I felt as if I was at the very edge of coming but Jenna wasn't going further and I knew it would be a while before I did come even if she said I could, she wasn't going to let me yet.

I stood and held her head as she bobbed up and down on it. After a few bobs Jenna tucked me back in my pouch and sheath and stood up before me. "What do you say we go get a drink and some treats on the patio?"

Jenna took me by the hand and we worked our way down the stairs and out onto a cobblestone patio. There was a conversation pit under a gazebo in the center. Jenna led us to the couch and we sat down.

I felt the warm breeze off the sunny section of the patio blow against my legs, further stimulating them. The butler showed up with a tray and a white towel over his black-coated arm. "May I get you ladies a drink?"

Jenna responded for the two of us. "Of course, two long island iced teas please? I'm sorry, I never got you name."

"Lady Jenna and Lady Yvette, my name is Collar since I arrange the guest list." He smiled, turned on his heel and went for the drinks.

I felt my skin tingle as I crossed my legs and arranged my dress over my tingling thighs. I looked at Jenna. "Collar? Arranging the guests and Roster tracking them? What kind of place is this?"

Jenna placed her silky hand on my knee and looked into my eyes with those bright blue jewels of hers. "Don't worry baby just enjoy the vacation. It's very different from anyplace we've ever been. That's why we're here."

Collar returned with the drinks in tall thin glasses with straws and an umbrella in each. He placed them before us on the coffee table, nodded and left. I took a sip. It was perfect with a hint of mint as well. My lipstick left a pretty pink ring on the straw.

Jenna tasted hers and we both sat taking in the beauty of the view from the patio. It looked out across an expanse of grass with clusters of trees, flowerbeds, a rose garden and a vine covered trellised walk. The air was fresh and clean and smelled with the scent of pine coming from the woods, which surrounded the grassy area. I finished my drink quickly, as did Jenna and Collar brought two more to replace them before we had even put the glasses on the table.

We sat quietly enjoying the scenery. I felt that luscious warm breeze blow up my dress and against my legs. I felt the pull of my breasts. I crossed and uncrossed my legs. I smoked a cigarette and Collar held the ashtray as I did and took it from me when I was done. I was starting to feel the effects of the alcohol as it loosened me up. Jenna held my hand now. "Feeling better? A little more relaxed?"

"Yes, thank you. Much better."

"Good. So Yvette, how do you feel now in that body? What would you like to do with it?"

"I feel incredible. Do with it? I'm not sure what you mean."

"Well, you love to watch me come right? What is it that makes that so enticing to you?"

"YOU do. I mean seeing you have all that pleasure."

"Do you ever think about what it feels like for me?"

"Always. I sometimes wish I could be you to be able to feel it."

"That's what I thought. That's why you like the fantasy of seeing me have a man. You like to imagine what it feels like. Am I right?"

"Uh, I guess I may have had that thought before of course. How could I not?"

"Of course dear, how could you not? It wouldn't be human if you didn't have it. Humans wonder and imagine constantly. So that means it's only natural for you to want to see me do that since that is human nature to wonder and imagine." Jenna leaned over on the couch and waved for Collar to come over. His long lean form strolled gracefully over with his white towel on his arm. He stood before us. "Collar, could you please move the coffee table aside and stand in front of Yvette?"

"Of course Lady Jenna." Collar moved the table and stood before me.

"Move closer now Collar. Right up to the seat."

Collar moved up till his pants touched my leg and I uncrossed them and folded them to the side. He moved in closer till his legs touched my knees.

"Good. Now take your cock out and present it to Yvette. She wants to suck it."

Collar stood before me, unzipped his pants and pulled out a real man's cock, a gorgeous real man's cock. I looked up at him and he smiled at me as he held it for me. I wrapped both hands around the semi hard cock and looked at how pretty my nails looked against the velvety flesh with the massive tube running under it that would jettison his come out of it. The head was almost fully purple and the hole in the head was large enough for a pencil to go in. I stroked it and wrapped my lips around it. It felt as if it had it's own electricity in it that made my tongue tingle as I now bobbed up and down on it and felt it grow further in my mouth.

I looked over with my eyes at Jenna as I sucked it and Jenna smiled and stroked my hair as I did. "That's it Yvette, make Collar good and hard for me so you can watch him fuck me." I looked back at Jenna with my eyes wide open while I sucked him. I got more excited each second thinking about watching him fuck Jenna. My cock throbbed under my dress and did a little dance and felt incredible. Collar started to push into my head holding me with both hands and I took this as a good indication that he was ready and my anticipation couldn't wait anymore to see this monster inside of Jenna..

I released him, stood up and moved to a seat across from the couch. As I did, Jenna took Collar by the hand as she lay back on the couch with her legs spread and ready for him. She guided him into her dripping slit as he spread her wide and her eyes rolled back in her head and she moaned. "Ungh! Now that's a cock! Fuck me Collar! Fuck me hard so Yvette can see me come on your cock!" Jenna looked at me, grinned an evil grin and winked as Collar began shoving his cock into her hard and fast. Jenna's head moved in time with his thrusts as her right hand pulled at his thick black hair and her left hand squeezed his hard ass through his pants making him thrust deep and hard.

My own cock was at the edge of coming under my dress as my senses went on overload watching Jenna. I could almost feel Jenna's penetration with each thrust. As I saw the thick, wet, shiny, purple, head embraced by Jenna's lips as it exited, I felt the tip of my body tingle in the anal area. I then saw the head enter and spread her lips back open with the thick wet meat of Collar. I could almost feel a filling up inside of myself.

Collar pulled down Jenna's top and bra below her breasts exposing and lifting them. He hunched over and took one of Jenna's breasts fully into his mouth as he continued to thrust in and out. I could feel his wet warm sucking on my own breasts. Collar moved his head away and squeezed that now wet breast with his big hand while he held Jenna to the couch with the other huge hand pushing back one leg. I could feel his hands on myself as I sat back in a similar position imagining the feeling as I held my gel breast in my hand.

Jenna looked over at me with one eye as she shuddered with orgasm and licked her lips. Her eyes then locked onto Collars as her hands held fast to Collar's ass through his pants. "Fuck me harder with that gorgeous cock Collar. Fuck me like you never fucked before while I squeeze you inside of me!"

Collar sped up and slid her down some to be able to get all nine inches of his thick cock into Jenna. He crushed her thigh in his hand as his cock glistened going in and out. Jenna squirted all over him and his pants as she came a second time with Collar not slowing or letting up a bit.

Collar was feeling the urge to come now and it showed on his face as he sped up even faster and banged into Jenna so hard the heavy couch was sliding across the stone of the patio. Jenna's head was bobbing against the back of the couch as Jenna called out in a cry to Collar. "That's it, come inside of me you fucking stud! Ung! Ungh, ungh! Feels...sooooo. Fucking good!"

Collar tensed up. "Oh God! This come is going to be huge! Ungh! Fuck Yea! Tight fucking pussy! Ungh! You have such a hot, tight cunt!" Collar SLAMMED his huge hard dripping cock into Jenna and held it there for a second. His face was contorted and flushed like Jenna's now. He then pulled back but not out and shoved it in again.

Twelve times he did this with each surge of his orgasm. I could imagine feeling Jenna's pleasure myself with each of those thrusts. Under my dress, without even touching myself, I came in time with Jenna's third orgasm on Collar's cock. I felt the come splash on my stockings and soak into my sundress through my panties. It felt like a quart of come was flooding out of me. Collar pumped into her filling her deeply until he and I were both spent.

Collar collapsed on Jenna. Jenna then released him and pushed him on the chest to get him off. Collar pulled out, his come oozed from Jenna and he twitched and shuddered as he slipped the head out trailing come over Jenna's leg. He stood, put his cock in his pants, picked up his white towel, nodded and smiled at us both and left.

Jenna smiled that smile of utter satisfaction and rearranged her clothes. She looked at me and asked how it was.

"It was incredible. It must have felt awesome for you."

"It sure did baby. See how good a real man sized cock feels when he can keep pounding it in for that long? There is nothing that can compare to that feeling! Nothing!! I think it's time for you to get to experience having a cock enter you and make you come on it this week. Ready to eat? Your appetizer is on your legs and mine and inside of me."

Watching and Brian

I was half asleep dreaming of Jenna and Collar. I smelled Jenna's perfume and heard her moaning softly and whispering. I could hear the low voice of Collar as he responded. "Ummm, yea, that feels good baby. I think I'm ready to do it again."

"Well that's a good Collar because that's exactly what I want," Jenna whispered in my dream. I saw Collar as he entered Jenna and Jenna whispered to him, "Oh yea!" I felt the bed start to shake as I lied on my side, my cock now in my hand wrapped in the satin of my nightgown dreaming of Jenna and Collar. I opened my eyes and realized it wasn't a dream.

I saw Collar's sinewy butt clench and relax as he thrust into Jenna. He held her down by her black strappy high heels. Both of them were totally naked except for Jenna's shoes. His shaved, smooth, skin appeared silky to the touch. His wet hair and fresh smell along with Jenna's wet hair told me that they had showered. He then released her heels and wrapped his arms around her back crushing her breasts between them. His fingers clenched her hair as he kissed her deep on the lips while sliding his cock in and out.

Jenna had one hand in his hair pulling him to her mouth and one hand clenching his bottom. She dug her nails into his flesh and made him thrust at the pace she wanted. They broke the kiss as Jenna whispered breathily, "I'm coming again baby. Keep going just like that! Oh that's it. Yes!" Jenna pushed her head back into the black satin pillow and looked

Collar in the eyes while both of her hands squeezed his butt and pulled him deep inside her with each thrust. Collar squeezed her in his bear grip of a hug as he fucked her and locked eyes with her.

Jenna was coming now as she made quiet throaty sounds and Collar grunted as he filled her with come again. Jenna then breathily spoke. I could hear her clearly. "Oh Collar, I fucking love your real man cock! It feels so damn good!" As they both came together I let out a little yelp as I came violently in my nightgown. Jenna heard me and looked over. "Oh baby, so glad you woke up for that! I didn't want to wake you but I also wished you could see and hear this for yourself again. Did you come good?"

I nodded and smiled as I licked the come off my fingers and sucked it from my nightgown as Jenna had taught me. Jenna looked back at Collar and wrapped her legs around his ass as she basked in the afterglow squeezing him inside of her. Collar winked at me and laid his torso alongside Jenna while he relaxed.

They both dozed off for a while, as did I. When I woke, Jenna was finished showering again and she was naked, lying alongside me, wrapped around my body, spooning me from behind. Her hand was sliding over my cock through my nightgown. She whispered in my ear. "Mmm, I still say your cock is cute! I love you Yvette! We need to get you satisfied like I've been lately."

"Honey, I'm not so sure I could take a cock up my bottom like that. I mean, it's so big!"

"Sweetie, of course it can't happen just like that. We'll have to get you in shape for it. We have to prepare you. So, today, after we eat and you shower, I want you to use the attachment we have in the shower to clean yourself out down there a little. Then we can start getting you in shape so it won't hurt you."

"Do I have to? I really think I can just continue to come masturbating. Why do I need someone in there?"

"Because you're going to want to feel it. You'll see, you'll be begging me for someone to do it to you once you get in shape for it. We started before with this but never really got anywhere. You remember how sensitive it is in there and how good it felt when I stimulated it for that hour. And, each of those ten second milkings you couldn't wait for each day. Now it's time to get it done. Go have some breakfast and shower. Collar brought it up for us and it's on the table by the windows. I'll pick out your clothes for the day."

I sat and ate cold poached eggs with capers, fresh baked bread, two grapefruit halves and a kiwi. I took my vitamins with some orange juice and took my pink pill as well. After a cup of coffee and a couple of cigarettes I went into the bathroom.

I did my thing and shaved and showered. I used the attachment, which Jenna asked me to use. It actually felt quite nice having that water running inside of me caressing my prostate and having all the mess go away. I felt clean and fresh inside and out.

I dried my hair and did my makeup. The new hairstyle was so easy to do with the layers and the way it just fluffed out and framed my face. The highlights ,in combination with the cut, gave it all a textured, wilder look.The makeup went on quick and easy now that I knew what I was doing and it accented all my best feminine features. My lips looked kissable and like lips that any man would want wrapped around his cock, which is good because I was starting to love sucking cock! I smoothed a floral scented body lotion over my body and felt the sensual caress my hands gave me as I did.

On the bed Jenna had left my outfit and a small vibrating butt plug with an inflator on it to increase it's size once inside me. I guess this is what would put me in shape for what Jenna thought I would want but I couldn't imagine it working. I took the plug into the bathroom and inserted it. I connected the inflator and pumped it up till I felt it fill me to a little more than was immediately comfortable. I then disconnected the inflator and turned on the vibrator, which gave me a very pleasant feeling there. I reattached the inflator and pumped it up further which only seemed to make it feel even better. I started to remember the feeling of the milkings again and how good they felt. I stopped inflating it and disconnected the hose. I went back into the bedroom.

Standing by the couch was a petite, pretty woman in a maid's outfit. She had a short maid's dress with a deep plunging V-neck, which exposed her perky full breasts completely to the hard nipples which peeked above the fabric. She smiled from beneath her red bangs as I approached. "Lady Yvette. I'm here to help you get ready. Please sit on the couch and put your feet on the ottoman so I can paint your toenails." Her tiny, unassuming, delicate, voice so pleasant to hear.

She held out a short pink satin robe for me, wrapped it around me and tied the sash. I seated myself and she began to work on my feet. First she massaged them with a lotion that seemed to remove all the dead skin. Then she massaged some scented lotion on them. It all felt wonderful! She manicured my toenails and cuticles. Then she painted them with a hot pink polish all the while smiling up at me.

When she was done with my toes she did my hands the same way. Then she checked my ear piercings and cleaned them inserting new earrings in them. They were silver shoulder dusters with pink feathers in them and the other pair was silver hoops about four inches in diameter. She commented on my piercings. "You'll have to get more, maybe one in the ear up top on each. You have such pretty ears. After you get those you might want more."

"More? Where would I have room?"

She smiled at me as I looked at her freckles and bright green eyes. Her ruby lips parted and a pink tongue shot out which showed me a piercing through her tongue. There was a silver ball on the top and bottom where her tongue was pierced through. "See, like this!"

"What good is that? No one can even see it."

"Oh, it's not for seeing but for feeling. Let me show you. By the way, my name is Prepper since I prepare people." She now pushed the ottoman aside and spread my legs.

She maneuvered herself between them and lifted my nightgown. She took my cock into her mouth. She started with running her tongue around the shaft and I could feel the hard steel ball make circles around it. Then she bobbed her head up and down on it and I felt the ball on the underside of my cock. Then, she moved her head around to get the proper angle and I felt the ball run across the opening at the tip. I shuddered and tensed each time she did it. She pushed the ball inside of the head and out.

The sensation of the plug in my bottom and this was too much for me and it didn't take long for me to come powerfully in her mouth, which she swallowed happily. After coming 16 times a day before and getting used to it I had a good 14 more in me at least so why not. It wasn't taking me long to get hard again, that's for sure. She looked up and wiped some come off her chin and licked her finger smiling at me. "See, that is what that piercing is for. Nice isn't it? The men love it. Was it good for you?"

"Yes, Prepper, incredible! Thank you." Prepper continued to look me over. She checked my face and hands. She looked at my arms and legs.

"I think next time I will start with some electrolysis on some of your face and then work around your body getting the little hair that you do have removed permanently so it's easier for you in the morning and you'll be smoother. The men like really smooth. Now we dress you."

Prepper stood me and walked me over to where my clothes were laid on the bed. She took the white and pink satin garter belt and wrapped it around me fastening the hooks behind me. She then seated me on the bed while she took the sheer white stockings and knelt on the floor. She kissed my feet, admired her paint job and rolled one stocking up in her hand and slid it over my foot. She smoothed it up my leg stretching it as she went and connected the six garters to it. She adjusted the ribbons on them to cover the clasps as she finished each one. She did the same to the other leg.

The feeling of the silky sheer stockings and her hands on my legs made me hard once more and it stood out before her. She looked at it and smiled then looked at me. "Shall I do it again?"

"No thanks Prepper. I think I'll just enjoy it as it is right now but thanks for asking."

Prepper continued to dress me as she stood me up and kissed and sucked my nipples and then wrapped a white and pink satin bra around me. She inserted my 34 C gel forms into them and adjusted my flesh to make a nice cleavage. Then she put a silver necklace with pink feathers on it around my neck and adjusted the length to lie just between my breasts in the valley of my cleavage.

Prepper held a pair of pink and white satin, crotchless panties out for me and helped me step into them. She slid them up my legs and over the garter straps adjusting my parts so they were framed by the panties. There was a wide satin ribbon hanging from the waist, which she wrapped under my globes and tied a bow in. They were now held up and presented forward. My cock throbbed in the air above it.

She kissed my wrists and hands and slid pink and silver bracelets on my wrists. She put a silver and pink feather clip in each side of my blonde hair and then put a silver ear cuff on my left ear. She knelt and kissed my ankle before putting a silver anklet with the letters S, L, U, and T hanging from it. She kissed the other ankle and put another silver anklet on it this time with my name in letters hanging from it.

"You have such a pretty body, cute little cock and such lovely legs. Everyone will fall in love with you. I think you will be the most popular."

She had me sit so she could slip on a pair of strappy pink and white five-inch high heels with the heels so thin I thought they might break. There was a pink and white flower on each foot by the toes, which perfectly matched the color of my toenails beneath the sheer white hosiery. She put the ankle strap through the buckle and pulled it snug. She pushed the pin into the hole in the strap and slid the strap under the buckle. She did the other foot.

She took the dress from the bed and had me step into it. It had pink flowers on white cotton. It was a bubble hem dress with two ruffles at the hip and a silky feeling lining under a crinoline lining. She adjusted the straps to cover my bra strap and adjusted the front to allow my cleavage to show. She fluffed the hem out so the bubble of the dress flared out about a foot above my knee.

Prepper then sprayed perfume on my stockinged legs and sprayed my breasts and hair, She took the pink pocketbook from the bed and put my lipstick, perfume, cigarettes and lighter, brush and comb, a small bottle of pink pills and blue E.D. pills and a few packs of non lubricated rubbers in it. She looked at me and handed me the purse. "Here you go Yvette. All ready for the day. Go enjoy it!" She kissed me on my cheek and pointed me toward the door. I almost felt like my mom was getting me ready for my first day of school!

I went out the door and down the spiral staircase. Each step I took down the stairs, I felt the tip of my cock rub against the soft silky lining under the dress. My skin was tingled and I felt the slip of the stockings against my skin with each step I took.

My breasts bounced on each step and the pull of the bra straps felt good. I wondered if having implants wouldn't really feel better yet. The thought gave me a rush of excitement over doing it all, as Jenna had suggested, and getting that done along with everything else. If I was having surgery anyway I might as well have my butt and hips done too. Oh my God! What was I thinking!

When I reached the bottom of the stairs I saw a line of men waiting to enter an office down the hall. There must have been twenty in line and more milling around waiting to get in line. Roster was walking past in his usual attire. I waved at him and he came over.

"Yes Lady Yvette, how may I help you?" He flashed his white teeth at me and tilted his head inquisitively.

"Roster, what is the line for? Why are there so many people? Men as well, only men."

"That's for the checking in process and the place they're waiting to get into does the testing. It's a precaution to keep everyone safe."

"I see, thank you!" I smiled and touched his shoulder as I moved on toward the patio. Men were milling about everywhere. Handsome, good looking men of all sizes. Testing must be some sort of security procedure. I clicked my spiky heels across the marble floor. I heard them click with each minced step I took. The heels made my hips sway as I walked which then made me rub beneath the dress some more. I was floating in an island of sensation as I walked smelling the scent of my perfume like the flower I was dressed as.

I took a seat on a bar stool in the shade of the bar's roof and crossed my legs looking around me. It was now one o'clock and the bartender came over to offer me a drink.

"Lady Yvette can I get you a drink? Maybe a mimosa, or a cape coder or an iced tea?"

"I think an iced tea with lemon, unsweetened would be good. Not a long island iced tea just an iced tea please. Have you seen Jenna?"

"Jenna was here earlier but she said she had quite a few meetings scheduled and if I saw you I was to tell you so so you wouldn't be concerned. She said she would see you later and don't forget to take you pink pill." He turned and went about fetching the drink for me.

I opened my purse and watched as my beautifully manicured long nails went into it and took out the bottle of pink pills. I opened it and took one. Heck, why not, it feels good. I lit a cigarette and enjoyed the sensualness of the smoke as it flowed in and out of me while I bounced one leg over the other and felt my thighs in stockings caressing me. The temperature felt like a perfect seventy-five degrees. The smell of the air was fresh and clean with a hint of pine from the woods. The thing in my bottom hummed gently along though it couldn't be heard only felt. I was ready and able to come again anytime. If I was to keep up with my previous pace that is.

The bartender brought my iced tea with lemon and a sprig of spearmint. It smelled wonderful and tasted refreshing. I looked around at all the men. Why were they all here? It's a Sunday afternoon. Maybe this is some sort of gay men's club or some kind of country club for men. They all were good looking even in the bathing suits some of them wore or the summer silk pants and shirts. I saw a shorter man like I was before I put a dress on and wondered if he had the same issues I used to. It almost seemed he heard me as he turned his head and came over to me.

"You must be Lady Yvette. I know you're on vacation today so I don't mean to bother you but I had to meet you. Mind if I join you?"

He looked at me with his brown eyes and longer, almost shoulder length, blonde hair swept to one side. His shorts hid his manhood but his lack of shirt and other clothing showed a body free of hair, in firm shape, not over built but firm and shapely. He was a handsome guy at about five foot four with two diamond stud earrings in each ear.

"Sure, have a seat."

"So Jenna is your wife? You are a lucky girl."

"Thanks. I think so too. She has a busy day of meetings though so I doubt I'll get to see her till later."

I turned to lean on the bar and my foot accidentally touched his leg. He turned in his seat to face me and put his bare feet on the rail of my chair. I turned in my seat slightly to face him and ended up touching his leg with mine but he didn't retract from it. He actually let his leg apply a little more pressure against mine. My leg tingled where he touched it and my heart raced a little with the novel feel of a man's leg against mine and the thought of him actually being interested in me as a woman.

I was wondering if he knew what I really was when he looked at me holding his iced tea in his left hand and he put his right hand gently on my knee leaning in to whisper to me. "I can't believe how good you look. I've often wondered if I shouldn't do the same! Do you think I could?"

That answered my question. But how did everyone know about Jenna and I? "Yes, thank you. Jenna let me learn that this is how I was really meant to be. I uh," I looked at him up and down. "I uh, I think you would transform pretty well though you have much more muscles than I. They would fade once you stopped working out though. Do you have a problem with making women come?"

He laughed and looked around before he opened his shorts to show a cock twice the size of mine and it wasn't even hard yet. "What do you think?"

"Uh, it might be hard to hide that under a skirt. Ha ha ha. Very nice. You are lucky."

"Thanks! If you get bored later you're welcome to take a closer look."

I felt myself throb at the thought of it and the thought made me shift in my seat. My leg ended up pressing harder against his and I slid it up and down some to see his reaction.

"Your stockings feel so nice against my leg. Thank you."

I let my leg slip back and forth against him now as I smiled at him. He was cute and interested in me. What a strange feeling that gave me! As I ran my leg across his, I glanced down at his shorts, which now no longer hid his manhood as it pressed against the loose fabric trying to get out. I felt myself throb against my dress again just thinking about how I was exciting him so easily. I finished my iced tea and decided I should have something to relax me.

The bartender came back. "Another iced tea?"

"Oh, no, I think I'd like a long island iced tea if I could this time."

"Same for me!" My new friend said. Then I realized I hadn't gotten his name.

"I'm sorry I never got your name." I leaned into him, offered my hand and slipped both my legs against his. The palm of his left hand slid along my legs as his right hand came out to shake mine.

"My name is Brian. Nice to meet you Yvette."

"My pleasure I'm sure." I shook his hand and put my other hand on his on my knee and motioned for him to keep caressing my leg, as it felt so darn good. He did and he moved his barstool closer to mine as we both now faced the bar. His hand went into my lap and mine into his. I ran my hand over his shaved, smooth, legs and slipped a nailed finger under the cuff of his shorts where I was able to flick the end of his cock gently. He moved closer against me and found me through the dress as I found him from outside his shorts. He was hard as a rock and quite large.

I felt his hand wrap around my cock and he looked into my eyes. "It's cute! I love it! But I really shouldn't be bothering you. You're on vacation."

"Nonsense, what else could vacation be for? Ha ha ha."

"That's why I'm here, for a little vacation. Like to go for a little walk around the grounds? The weather is as gorgeous as you are." He removed his hand from my lap and put it on the back of my chair while he waited patiently. I lifted my hand from his lap and grabbed my new drink. I sipped from the straw and looked into his eyes as I did. What was I doing? Is this what Jenna was thinking I would do? It isn't what I would have thought I'd do a few weeks ago, that's for sure. But the way I'm feeling now is entirely different.

I sipped another sip, smiled hesitantly and looked at him again as he waited for my response. I must have made him less confident since he responded before I could. "I'm sorry, like I said, you're on vacation so forget I even said it."

That got me. I knew now I didn't want to stop where we were going. "No! No! No! I'm sorry, I was just lost in thought." I placed my hand back in his lap and could tell he had softened some but he welcomed my hand back with a throb and he put his hand on top of mine and pushed his cock against it. "Yes, a walk would be nice. Thanks for asking. How about we finish our drinks, I go to the ladies room and then we can walk around."

"That sounds super!" He slugged on his straw and ran the tea down half empty. I did the same. I was so nervous and excited. I had to maximize this experience. I opened my purse and took out the bottle of pink pills. I took one more. Then I took out a cigarette, which he lit for me with my lighter. I could feel the effects of the first pill from earlier and couldn't wait to feel the second one.

My skin tingled and each time he touched me I felt as if that part of my body was close to orgasm. His hand slid up and down from my crossed knee to my thigh to just under the hem of the dress. It felt like a dream. "I love the feel of your stockings. They're so smooth and silky on your skin. The white color makes you look so innocent, virginal, and yet tremendously hot and sexy."

"Thank you! I'm glad you like them. I think your legs would look nice in stockings and heels. You have such smooth, hairless, tan legs. And your height is like mine so you wouldn't be too tall in heels." I leaned over to whisper in his ear and squeezed his cock. "But this would be difficult to hide. Have you ever been dressed?"

"Oh, I have enjoyed the pleasure some. Yes, it's nice isn't it? Maybe I can dress for you sometime if you're interested."

"That sounds like fun!" I finished my drink, slurped the bottom with the straw and looked at the bartender. "We're going to go for a walk. Do I owe you anything or is this on a tab?"

"Oh no Lady Yvette. You need not worry about paying for anything here. Please, have another!" He smiled and nodded. I looked at Brian. He shrugged his shoulders and slurped his drink down with the straw. I could feel the second pink pill kicking in, but the feeling of the long island iced tea with the five shots in it felt good as well. What the heck, I'm on vacation, so what if it's one thirty in the afternoon. I nodded and pointed at our glasses and the bartender was off to make two more.

Brian looked at me as he continued to caress my leg and drive me crazy. "I hope your not trying to get me drunk and take advantage of me. Ha ha ha."

"Oh, why would you say that? The man is the one that takes advantage of the woman. I think it might be your doing."

"I didn't order the drink, Yvette, you did."

"Oh, yea of course. In that case then, I guess I must be trying to take advantage of you."

Roster walked by with his clipboard and stopped momentarily after seeing Brian and I. He made a note, looked at his watch and made another note. Then he said hello. "Hi Brian and Lady Yvette. Enjoy your day!" Roster went on his way.

We enjoyed our drinks and then Brian and I both had a cigarette. When we were done I Brian led me to to the ladies room and he went to the men's room.

I struggled peeing due to my hard on but got done and I slipped a rubber on so I wouldn't have an accident and mess my dress or waste any come. I was so on the edge I felt I could come just walking in this dress and heels. I could never have imagined this feeling so damn good before.

I stood before the mirror, touched up my mascara and eyeliner then added a little blush and freshened my lipstick. I sprayed some of the perfume into my hair, and on my legs and shoulders. I then watched my long fingernailed hands take the flowers out of my hair. I brushed my hair out and put the flowers back in. I looked into the mirror and felt as if I was looking at someone else but when I moved, they moved. It was as if I was outside of my body but my body was a gorgeous woman.

My cleavage was perfect as was my makeup and hair. I turned and looked into the full-length mirror. Gorgeous! I never would have cared to take so much time in the mirror before. This was actually quite entertaining, as was having a man's interest and being able to get him aroused so easily. This should be an interesting walk.

A Little Picnic With Refreshments

Brian was now wearing an opened, button down shirt and held a blanket under his arm and a picnic basket. "Lunch! We should eat, it's past lunch time, and I have a thermos with more tea too." He held the basket up momentarily to show me and then reached for my hand to lead me outside again. I slung my purse over my shoulder, flicked my hair back gently with my long nails and took his warm, soft, hand in mine

We walked across the marble floor inside and then the stone of the patio. I felt all the rush of sensations of course and they were now more intense than the first time I took the pink pill. I opened my purse while we walked and I couldn't resist taking another. Jenna did say I couldn't overdose on them and it just kept getting better. I slipped the purse off my shoulder and quickly dug out the bottle and took two more while we walked.

Brian commented on the pills. "Are you okay? I mean, do you have a headache?"

"Oh no, these are just, uh, for, uh, actually, they're a libido enhancer. Want one?" I held the bottle out to him. He smiled and took two himself.

"Mmm, candy coated. Not that my libido needs any help with you near me but what the heck huh?" He handed the bottle back and it rattled as I put it back in my purse.

We reached the asphalt path that led into the shaded woods. There were little alcoves set back off the path that were fairly private. Brian stopped at one ,unfolded the blanket and set it out on a soft bed of pine needles. He took out some plates and arranged shrimp cocktail, cocktail sauce with lots of horseradish, and crackers. He put a teaspoon of caviar on each of two crackers; the little red balls oozed a little red salty juice, which made my mouth water. Then he sliced up a crisp granny green apple and some Stilton blue cheese on another plate. He then took out a split of Port wine for the desert to go with the apples and cheese. I then realized I was hungry.

"There, a table set for Lady Yvette. Please, have a seat." He looked up at me and patted the blanket. I seated myself folding my legs to the side beneath me and adjusted the bubble hem of my dress as I sat. I pointed my toes out and straightened my ankle as if posing. Somehow that felt natural to me as if you couldn't just leave your foot there at a nondescript angle. I put my purse down and flicked my hair back with a couple of fingernails as Brian seated himself.

Brian sat like an Indian with his legs crossed which allowed me to see he was still hard in his shorts. I felt myself throb beneath the dress thinking about it and looking at it. Brian poured us some long island iced teas from the thermos into some tall glasses and put a straw in each of them. He handed one to me. "What would you like first. Maybe some shrimp?" He held one by the tail and dipped it into the sauce. He held his hand beneath it as he brought it to my lips.

"Oh, you're going to feed me?"

"Why not! What could be more fun that that." He dangled the shrimp temptingly before me as my stomach rumbled and I opened my mouth. He put it in and I didn't bite it but let it slip back out between my lips. I tasted the cocktail sauce. I flicked my tongue at it as it left and was still held in Brian's fingers..

"Mmm, good sauce!" I reached for the shrimp with my tongue again and he held it before me as I licked at it with my tongue. Then I bit it off at the tail.

"Yikes! You nearly got my finger! Ha ha."

Brian went for a cracker with the caviar and fed me that now. The crunch of the cracker and the squish of the eggs contrasted as the salt filled my taste buds. "Mmm," I said as I rolled the combination around in my mouth. I never realized how sensual food could be. Was it the pink pills? I watched as Brian ate a shrimp himself then got another ready for me.

We ate lunch that way, as we smelled the fresh forest air scrubbed clean from the pine trees. Squirrels rummaged through the leaves for mushrooms and pine nuts. A hawk circled overhead where he screeched his supremacy and looked for his next meal. Red and green cardinals sang while a woodpecker rapped away at a hollow tree. It was gorgeous there.

We finished our long island iced teas and I was feeling a good buzz at that point. Brian opened the desert, a port wine, and poured two small wine glasses of it. He proceeded to feed me crisp, tart Granny Green apples and buttery Stilton blue cheese. The combination of port, fruit and the cheese was magnificent. I didn't really need any more alcohol but the port was too good to pass up!

When we were done, Brian took out an ashtray and I opened my purse and got us a couple of cigarettes and a lighter. Brian took them from me and lit them. He handed the first one to me. "Thank you!" I blew the smoke out French inhaling it through my nose. The sensation of the smoke was as good if not better than the whole lunch. "Mmmm!!" I took another drag and blew the smoke out between pursed lips. "Ffff." I felt it against my lips. "That was sooo good. Thanks for thinking of that Brian. So how long are you on vacation? Will you be staying here for a while?" I slid my leg over the other beneath my dress and felt my stockinged legs slide against each other while the garters pulled on them. I put my palm over my cock and pressed on it feeling the precome in the rubber making the head slip and slide inside. I twitched as I did.

"I'll be here for some time."

"Would you like to join us for dinner tonight?"

"That would be great! Should I, uh, dress for dinner? You know, be Briana?"

111

"Now that would be fun to see. I'd love to see you that way. It would give me some company in my specialness as well since I've never met anyone like that." I slid over on the blanket and got alongside of Brian now and he put his hand on my knee. I put my hand on his crotch as I looked him in the eye. He was hard and throbbed for me letting me know he was interested in more as was I. "Please come as Briana."

"Then I will." Brian put his hand under my dress and found my cock, which he stroked with the rubber and it made me push against him asking for more. I undid the belt on his shorts, unzipped them and he helped me as he slid them off revealing a lace men's thong, that showed the full size of him.

I slid my palm in the thong and slid the fabric under his globes and began to stroke him. I looked at my hand with the long hot pink fingernails and saw that my hand only covered half the length of it as my fingers wrapped around the velvety, hard, throbbing rod. My mouth watered in anticipation of having that velvety monster in my mouth. I had to have it! Just like Jenna said. I would beg for it. I had to pull Brian's hand off my cock or I would have come any second.

I leaned over and took the oozing tip in my mouth and ran my tongue in circles around it and tasted the salt in the precum. Brian twitched and tensed as I did and I felt his hand hold my head on it. He pushed it in further and I started to bob my head up and down. I felt the velvet of his cock skin as it slid over my lips and tongue. I could feel his electricity in my mouth whether it was from the pink pills or, just his cock and his energy. It felt like my tongue and lips were going to have an orgasm any second.

I lay down on my side and Brian didn't have much of a choice but to do the same as I held fast to his cock with my hand and mouth. I fed on it like a sex-starved slut as he began to thrust his hips while he held my head. He fucked my face like that, slowly at first. We must have done it for quite a while since I lost track of time and was lost in a blissful ride with that feeling and the rest of my body following in the tingle and excitement.

My ass was alive with the plug vibrating inside of it. My head spun from the alcohol but I was still not drunk, just in heaven.

Brain continued to fuck my face and I couldn't help but wonder what a cock like this would feel like inside of me with me on my back. Brian finally started to go faster and thrusted deeper to the point I gagged at first but then as I adjusted my neck angle I found I could take him right into my throat. As I did so he got more excited and I could hear him moaning as he approached the edge of no return. I was feeling similar myself as he started to vocalize his pleasure for me. "Oh yea. Ungh, ungh, ungh, Yvette, ungh feels, so, so, ungh, coming!"

Brian came in gush after gush and I tasted the salty, slightly sweet, thick liquid as I captured each gush and swallowed it greedily. I felt myself come in time with him as he did and I filled my rubber as I tensed. I felt as if my whole body was a cock coming. The plug in my bottom seemed to have an energy of it's own as I came clenching around it. A flood of come came out of both of us.

Mmm, it felt so delicious! I heard myself squeak out a breathless sound around his cock as he thrust his last four times into my face and throat. When it was over we stayed where we were and I could feel him going limp in my mouth. I gently caressed his cock with my tongue for the next few minutes and I felt myself soften and reharden again while I was doing so. I felt my rubber's tip filled with come hanging off the end.

As Brian removed his cock from my mouth, I opened my eyes. Brian stood and put his pants on. "I need to get ready for dinner. I'll see you there okay?"

"Okay. See you then!"

Brian walked away behind me and I lit a cigarette. When I looked up there was another gorgeous cock right in front of my eyes attached to a huge, six foot six maybe, smooth shaven, naked, olive colored guy with thick black hair. I saw Roster as he was just finishing writing on his clipboard and waved goodbye as this one held his cock, smiled at me and yet said nothing. I looked up at him and smiled back and he moved closer so I could even smell his cologne and I saw the precum on his cock as his huge hand stroked it in front of my face.

Then he spoke. "Lady Yvette, I know you're on vacation but after watching you and Briana I thought you might be willing to do the same for me. Of course if you'd rather not that's fine too."

"What the heck." I snuffed my cigarette out in the ashtray, wrapped my fingers and the long nails on them around his thick long velvet rod. I took his cock in my mouth while I stroked the remaining length of it. It felt similar to Brian's in many ways but was bigger and his hands were larger on my head. I knelt this time, held his cock with one hand, put my other hand on his muscular ass, and squeezed his ass cheek and gently dug my fingernails in.

I moved my hand that was on his cock down to his shaved balls, wrapped my thumb and forefinger around the two globes, and pulled them gently down while I bobbed my head up and down on him. I could smell his awesome smelling cologne on his skin as I licked my way down to his balls and took one in my mouth rolling it around while I stroked him. My hard cock under my dress was nearly ready to come again.

I went back up to the tip of his cock and circled it with my tongue, which made him quiver. I sucked his cock up and down and adjusted my neck angle to take him into my throat. He responded as he now fucked my face as he held my head firmly and I heard him moan in his deep low voice, "Coming!" Ungh YEA!!!" He came full force into me and spread my throat ten times before he finished.

As soon as he was done he pulled out, kissed me on the lips, said thanks and ran off. As I was turned around looking back at his gorgeous naked body running down the path another had taken his spot in front of me. When I turned back, a tall, black, shaved body, gorgeous hunk had his hard dick right in front of my mouth. He said one word. "Please!?" It came out in a deep voice while his eyes begged me and his flashing white teeth threw a gorgeous smile at me. I started on him.

I was becoming a connoisseur of cock and it felt wonderful! His was again a lot like the last two but also a lot different. His was thicker, harder, and had a bigger vein on the bottom like Collar had. It had softer more velvety skin than the others did. I felt everything he felt as I did him. My cock responded in like and we both came together.

No sooner was he gone than there was another in his place. Again, Roster was to the side taking notes and this time a short but handsome type with a cock at least as small as mine. It was easy to take him all the way in and he didn't even reach my throat. That allowed me to run my tongue around it and flick the tip over and over as I suckled it and bobbed on it. He'd lurch into my mouth each time my tongue passed over the tip and then pull back. He'd wait until I did it to him again and then lurch into my mouth again. I gently pulled on his sacks while my tongue ran around his shaft. He then held my head firmly and plunged over and over into my mouth and throat. When he came he seemed to have the most come of all of them and he nearly lost his balance as his legs went weak.

Well, needless to say, this went on for quite some time, one after another. I lost track of time until Jenna showed up and watched me do the last one. I had come seven times and my rubber beneath my dress was so full I had to tuck the end beneath the garter strap to keep it from falling off. Jenna wore running shorts and a tee shirt and appeared to have just finished running on the path. "Well, haven't you been a busy little girl! It must be feeling good for you or you wouldn't have done it. I hate to say I told you so but I told you so. This is what you are meant to be."

"Well, I think it might have something to do with the pink pills and the alcohol maybe."

Jenna picked up my purse and checked the bottle in it to see how many there were. "Well, if it was the pills, you consciously made a choice to take more of them because there are many more gone than would have been with the regular dosage. That tells me you wanted it."

"I guess."

"Now I bet you have a rubber on since your dress doesn't seem to be wet so take it off and drink it up so you don't lose it on the way back. How many did you suck today and how many times did you come out here?"

"Uh, I stopped counting at twelve and there were quite a few more. I came uh, at least seven times." I reached under my dress and took the rubber off being careful not to spill it. I spilled out my glass with the port wine into the pine needles and then squeezed the rubber into it. I looked up at Jenna and I drank the familiar taste and texture down.

"Good, that means you have gotten a super dose of libido enhancing testosterone. About the equivalent of raising your libido by another seventy percent from all that cock come, along with your own of course. Very good job dear. But if you came only seven times you probably have a good nine more in you for today based on what you were doing before in a day." Jenna squatted down and kissed me on the forehead and then held my hand to stand up. "Don't worry about the picnic things. Someone will be along to clean it up. It's time for you to get showered and changed for dinner. I hear we have a guest this evening by the name of Briana, another MTF like you but with a bigger cock."

"Uh, yea, I invited her, is that okay?"

"Of course sweetie of course. Let's go back in. Prepper should be ready for you since Briana went in earlier."

Three Girls For Fun

I took a shower and removed my butt plug. I felt sufficiently stretched by then but the feeling of it not being in almost made me put it back again. I left it out though thinking to myself that maybe something else might be going in there tonight. The thought made my cock leap to attention and my body tingled all over.

When I was done Prepper showed up. I redid my makeup at the makeup table while Prepper sucked my cock again. She did a great job of keeping me at the edge and not letting me come. Next, she smoothed a wonderful smelling body lotion all over me and stroked my cock with it. When she was done, we both went to the closet and I selected a dress.

It was black satin, down to my ankles in back and cut in a curved, rising hem from back to front to just below my pantie line. The hem had a cream colored ruffle around all of it which made a frame to display my legs. Prepper helped me put on a black satin garter belt that had six straps for each leg and had matching cream ruffles. Prepper picked out matching underwear for me along with six inch heeled, black satin, strappy sandals with a double ankle strap.

I took the dress to the bed and Prepper followed. She kneeled before me, sucked my cock again and then slid black, sheer, lace top stockings up my legs and attached them to the garters. Next, Prepper had me step into a pair of black satin, crotchless panties, again with the cream ruffle. The ruffle framed my balls and cock as the panty held them up and forward. Prepper then took an elasticized, wide black satin ring and held my globes, pulled them down, then she slipped this over them. This kept them gently stretch downward. The bottom of the ring had sheer black stocking like material, which encased my globes with shiny gold heart accents on it.

Next Prepper rolled a smooth, sleek, sheer, sheath over my cock. It matched the one over my globes and looked like a cock stocking but smoother and softer than a stocking. It formed to my hard cock sheathing it in silky splendor and my cock and balls now matched my stockings. Precum leaked from the tip through the sheer fabric. Prepper licked it off and slid a gold open-ended ring over my cock just under the head.

Prepper helped me put my bra on, inserted the gel forms into it, and adjusted them to make a lovely cleavage. I realized that I had actually missed the feeling of them and welcomed them back.

Prepper had me sit while she put the shoes on me along with gold ankle bracelets with little cocks hanging from them. I stood in the six inch heels and felt the height and tested them walking around. My steps were even more minced in them and they felt incredibly sexy. I could only take short strides but they felt so powerful!

Prepper held the dress for me. I stepped into it and raised it over my shoulders. She zipped the back and adjusted the straps to cover my bra straps. My sheer covered, decorated cock and balls lifted by the crotchless panties, stuck out from under the hem. Hmmm. I wasn't so sure I wanted to have it that way. I looked at Prepper and looked at my cock and she laughed, reached under the hem of the dress and dropped down another section of cream-colored ruffles which went down to cover my parts to just above the tops of my stockings. "Better?" she said, "If you want to get rid of it later just pull on it and it will come off. It has a few snaps holding it in place and they'll pop right off."

"Thanks Prepper."

Prepper sprayed my hair, arms, legs and breasts with perfume. She loaded a black and gold satin clutch for me with all of my things. She handed me two pink pills and a blue pill. "Jenna said you should have a blue pill tonight too so you can enjoy it even better." I took the pills and swallowed them down.

Prepper held out the matching black and cream ruffled, short sleeved, bolero jacket and I slid my arms through and put it on. She helped me put on some sheer, elbow length fingerless gloves and loaded my fingers with gold jeweled rings over the gloves. She put long dangling black and gold earrings in each of the holes in each ear. I heard them jingle as I moved.

Jenna came in the bedroom moving quickly with a man. She stripped her clothes off as she moved toward the bed. She got on top of the bed and spread her legs while the man, now also naked, got on top of her and fucked her like crazy. He did that for about five minutes. They both came and then he left unceremoniously. Jenna lay there and leaned on one arm with her head in her hand while she caught her breath. "Wow. That was a fast one. Did you like it?"

"Uh, yea, that was pretty hot. Did you really come that fast or was that just for show?"

"Heck no, that was for real! I've been coming like crazy! It's like a gate has opened! Don't get any ideas of you being able to do that though. You'd still come too fast in me. Let me get dressed and I'll see you downstairs. I think Briana is already in the sitting room off the dinning room. Go join her for a drink and I'll see you down there. Wow! That's a gorgeous dress! You should get rid of the ruffles in front though and let your pretty little decorated cock show. I got those cock clothes special so you can show it off."

"Okay, maybe later. See you down there sweetie."

Prepper had climbed on the bed and was fondling Jenna's breasts as she lay beside her as I went past them on the way out.

I walked down the spiral staircase as I carried my clutch and felt the blue and pink pills kicking in. My cock was rock hard now under the dress but completely concealed by the ruffles. I felt the stockings pull and slide on my legs with each forced, minced, step of the fantastic six-inch heels. When I reached the bottom of the stairs there was still a line at the hallway by the entrance. It seemed this place had a constant flow through security testing.

I turned the corner and down the hall and my shoes clicked on the marble floor echoing in the foyer. I found the study off the dinning room and Briana was in there reading a book on her iPhone when I walked in. Brian had transformed beautifully!

"Briana! You look incredible! Stand up so I can see all of you. My God you are gorgeous! Look at those boobs and your legs and face and hair! Wow! Awesome!"

"Thanks!" Briana gave a little spin showing herself off. Her black satin, bubble hem dress was a halter-top. The fabric was soft and thin and revealed her hard nipples. She had a cream colored ruffled portion that arched across the hem above her stocking tops like mine did.

"Are those gel forms?"

"Gel forms? These?" She grabbed her breasts and jiggled them, which flashed her gold painted nails on her long fingernail hands. "Uh, I have to confess something to you."

"No way, you didn't have them earlier. They can't be real."

"Well, you see, when I was young I discovered an ability I had. I was playing dress up with my mom's clothes when I was about 13 and I wished so much that I could look more like a woman and then, instantly, I grew boobs and hips and all of it. Of course, I learned how to go back and forth and learned that I couldn't make my cock go away but I could make it really small or really big. That's why I can have such a big one and be so short. I can't gain any height because bones don't stretch too easy but I can modify any fleshy portion. Watch!"

Briana pointed to her boobs and made them grow and shrink then she looked around and lifted her skirt showing me her now tiny erect cock that she had at the moment, framed by a pretty gold crotchless panty.

"Wow, how did you ever get so lucky! That's incredible! Maybe a little more hips and ass and less waist?"

Briana did as I asked. She looked like a little Barbie doll! A waiter came over to take drink orders. I ordered a pink cosmopolitan martini and Briana had the same. We sat on the leather sofa together and Briana finished her first drink. Her soft curvy hip was against mine as we sat. I crossed my leg and let it rest against her stockinged shapely leg. Where we touched, I tingled.

The drinks came and Briana and I toasted and sipped carefully so as not to spill them. Briana smiled at me and looked me over. "And you look ravishing! That dress is sooo hot! And those heels, to die for!" She kissed me on my lips, opened her purse and lit a cigarette for each of us leaving her pretty pink lipstick on each. I smelled the perfume on her wrist as she handed it to me and I grabbed it and kissed it there. "Mmmm, you smell luscious. I could eat you."

"You certainly could. I think I'd like that! I can make it any size you want too!"

I put my hand in Briana's lap and felt for her cock and it was tiny and hard and very cute right now. "I kinda like that yours is smaller than mine right now. Makes me feel superior. Ha ha ha. You don't have any other plans for tonight do you? I hope you can stay with me all night."

"All yours sister! I wouldn't want it any other way."

"Fabulous!" I ran my hand over her knee and caressed her leg. We sipped our drinks and enjoyed our smokes as we took in the ambiance of the mansion. This room was very manly with heavy, weathered leather, comfy chairs and sofas, hunter green walls with pictures of ducks in flight, animal heads on the walls and a gas fire burning in the fireplace even though it was summer.

There was a table between two comfy leather chairs with a chessboard built into it and ivory and ebony chess pieces. Another area had a green felt covered poker table in it. Across the room was a billiards table. In the corner, by the pool table, a stuffed polar bear stared at us with his arms reaching forward.

"Nice room, a little manly but impressive," Briana said. "Oh look, a case of cigars!" Briana leaned forward and opened the glass covered cigar box on the coffee table. She took out three of them and smelled them. "Mmm these will be good. I'll take three for after dinner for us and Jenna okay?"

"Sounds good."

Briana put them in her purse. She sipped her martini and put her hand in my lap. She wrapped her hand around me through the cream ruffles of my dress and began to stroke me gently and slowly.

"So sweetie, When is dinner. I'm getting a little hungry." She smiled an evil smile as she continued to caress me.

"Soon I hope. Jenna was getting ready and then I guess we'll eat next door. So tell me, what is with this place? That line for security testing is always full. There seems to be a constant stream of men through here."

Briana found the gold ring on the sheath over my penis with her hand and she pulled it up, which stretched my cock out and pulled on the head which made me twitch. "Stop! Ha ha ha. I don't want to come yet."

"Sorry, nice touch though. I like those too. Do you have the cock stocking on too?"

"Yes, Prepper took care of that for me. I love it."

"Sometime I wear one too but tonight I didn't want to for some reason. I just wanted my flesh against this silky dress. Prepper is great isn't she?"

"Wonderful! So tell me what is with that security testing and all these guys? Is it some kind of, uh, some kind of swingers club?"

Briana looked away and then back. She shifted and recrossed her legs so that one rubbed against mine as she bounced her foot. "Yea! That's it, a swingers club. That security check isn't for security dear. It's for S.T.D. testing. Everyone who comes here is checked each time they come here. They have a quick blood test and saliva test that tells us they're safe. So see, you don't have to worry about catching anything here since everyone is checked. Neat huh?"

"Very nice! I meant to tell you. After you left today, one guy after another showed up and stuck their cock in front of me just begging me to suck it. I don't know what came over me but I couldn't resist. I was a little worried with all the cocks I sucked today. Now I'm not. So do you enjoy all of this? I mean for guys, like we REALLY are, under all this girlie stuff, sucking a cock? Doesn't that make you feel weird?"

"It did at first, the first time I did it, which was probably when I was fifteen after I changed shape and went out dressed the first time. I had a little bit of an identity crisis of sorts after I switched back to male mode. But, since the guys were so taken with me though, I couldn't resist it. It seemed totally natural in fem mode."

"But didn't you think about it after, after you were done and not sexed up, didn't you feel weird?"

"Uh, a little maybe but no, not really. I think I realized that I could do whatever I wanted and really didn't feel like anything was too weird. It all felt good. There is nothing like making a guy crazy and bringing him to such a level of excitement that he comes. It's just as good as making a woman come. I like them both. How about you.?"

"Well, I never made a woman come with my cock so that is something I missed but making those guys come was really exciting, so much so, it seemed I was possessed! But I feel like such a liar. Like a fake after."

"Fake? There is nothing fake about you. You see how they enjoy it. Why shouldn't you feel good that you can do that? Especially if you can't make a woman come with your cock. My God! Enjoy girl!"

Briana ran her hand over my leg and her other hand moved the hair from my face. I almost felt like crying she made me feel so, so... I didn't know. I did feel she was a true friend of mine though. I loved Briana, so confident, in control, being whatever she is and not worrying about it.

"But Briana, don't you feel like a cheap slut when something like that carries you away. Don't you feel immoral? Especially knowing you're not a real woman even?"

"Immoral? Cheap? Not in the least and you shouldn't either. You're a goddess and that's how you should view yourself. No need to judge yourself in such an inexperienced manner. Just because you can do what you do and love it doesn't mean it's wrong. Wrong is society's word, not a goddess's. Love it, live it, enjoy it!" Briana brushed my hair back from my eyes, ran her hand over my head and looked into my watery eyes. "Don't be such a worry wart. Be who you are. Enjoy it."

"Hello ladies!" Came a call from Jeanna as she walked in minced, short, hip swinging steps in her six-inch heels. She came into the lounge with a dress the exact negative of mine. Black ruffles on cream and she had the front all the way up showing the lowest part of her sheer panties, the garters and stockings. She looked so hot. She wore the six inch heeled shoes like mine but in a cream color. She also had long hair somehow. Long, over the shoulder, black, shiny, wavy, thick hair!

I looked up at her as Briana and I cuddled together on the end of the sofa. "How did you do the hair?"

"Oh silly, it's a wig! Prepper weaved it in for me. It's completely attached. Pull it!" Jenna leaned down so I could pull her hair, which I did and it was tightly attached. It didn't come off and it looked so real! I never saw her without her short hair and she was as gorgeous as ever.

Jenna stood and smiled at us as she went on about her hair, her hands moving through it. "Yea, Prepper said that the guys like it like this, long and grab-able as opposed to my intense, manly like, short, gelled hair. I thought I'd give it a try for a few days. Do I look okay? It keeps getting in the way and in my mouth and eyes and it seems like a big pain in the ass! But if the guys like it, I guess it's worth it right girls?"

"Of course! They pay the bills right? Ha ha ha," Briana chimed in and then looked at me for my reaction as if she had not meant to say it.

Pay the bills? Strange she should say that to Jenna with what Jenna earns. I guess it was just saying what is normally a truth about men being the money makers. I looked at Jenna to see her reaction. She grabbed her dress and lifted the front. "Damn right baby! They fill the need too!! Woo hoo!"

I suspected we were in for a wild night. Jenna ordered a double shot of top label tequila, danced around sexy like a stripper till it came, gave the server a deep tongue kiss and rubbed his cock through his pants and then, she shot it down. She leaned over to me as I sat next to Briana and Jenna whispered in my ear, "Ready to watch your wife get pounded tonight? I'm soooo in the mood. You and Briana can play while I play. What do ya think sweetie?"

Why should she ask? She knows I like to see her and what could I do about it dressed like this anyway. Beside, she was right, I had Briana to keep me company. "Of course! Nothing I would want more than to see you and imagine that what's happening to you and the way you're feeling is actually me. What more could I want?"

"I didn't detect sarcasm in that response did I?"

"No, oh no sweetie. I mean it. I do have Briana here to keep me company. Please, please put on a sexy wonderful show for us."

Briana squeezed my hand and put her other one on my arm. "Jenna, of course I'd love to keep Yvette here company and enjoy your entertainment." She squeezed my hand as Jenna stood there rubbing her crotch as she smiled at us both.

"Thanks ladies, you two are so cute together!" Jenna adjusted her boobs so she maximized her cleavage and then she picked up her clutch and looked at us. "Hungry? Follow me girls." She clicked in her little steps across the wood floor to the dining room as we followed making a clatter of clicking heels.

Briana held my hand as we tried to get in time with each other's short wiggling steps and managed to do so finally when Briana held my arm in her hand and clutched me to her. She whispered. "Don't worry, this will be a great night for you and I...and for Jenna. Don't get nervous." I felt a throb under my dress that felt wonderful as my tingling body, held by Briana, entered the dining room.

Dinner With Appetizers Desert and Thankful Servants

We entered the dining room. We were the only ones there and there was a huge table that could seat about 40. Bach played through hidden speakers and filled the room with "Jesus Joy." The room was Victorian with a huge fireplace burning and the air conditioning running to keep up. Velvet seated chairs had carved arms and legs. Gold trimmed carpeted wall hangings showed pictures of hunting victories on the walls. Big-busted women with their cleavage showing knelt before their men as they served them reward drinks after they had unmounted their horses. I'm sure there were other rewards as well the way the women were dressed and probably some other kind of mounting.

Jenna had Briana and I sit at one end of the table while she walked down to the head of the table way at the other end. The chair there was more like a throne than a chair and she seated herself regally as a woman server came in. Briana moved her chair so that I could feel her leg slide against mine across the corner of the table.

The server was in a basic kind of submissive slave outfit but very classy. She had a gorgeous body, all maybe, five foot of her. She had her breasts captured in leather straps that held her firm and high and allowed the bulk of her breasts to be revealed. Her nipples were pierced and hard with a gold chain between them. Below her waist her lips were evidently trimmed away as there were none and there was a piercing just above her hard clit with a gold dangle that draped under her clit and a small cuff that it peeked out of.

She had wrist and ankle cuffs with fetish heels that made it darn near impossible to walk in. She had a butt plug in and a plug in front and both, I imagined, were vibrating. Her mouth was forced open by a device of some sort. She came over to Jenna. We heard Jenna greet her but no more. Jenna took the mouth device off her and kissed her deeply. She fingered her clit making her twitch. Then she said something to her and the little one ran off as best she could in her bindings. We all took in the room as we looked about it.

She came back so fast I couldn't believe it. She had an opened bottle of champagne and poured some for Jenna to test. When Jenna nodded her acceptance the server poured Jenna's and then came and poured each of us a glass. She then left the bottle by us. She then ran down the other end of the table, in her constrained little steps, and crawled under the table to get between Jenna's legs as Jenna moved about to find a comfortable position for the little submissive to eat her. The Bach played on at a comfortable back round level. Once she was positioned and Jenna was obviously enjoying it, Jenna spoke to us.

"Life is good isn't it girls? Mmm." I've ordered, ungh, yes little one, like that, uh, ordered us appetizers as well. Think of this evening as our launch evening for this week's vacation. I want you girls to want for nothing and fully enjoy it as much as possible. It should be a celebration of life and luxury." Jenna lifted her glass to us from across the room and we toasted her back as we both sipped the sparkling sweetness.

Out came the appetizers. Three very tall men, in black butlers outfits with Mardi Gras masks covering their faces, approached each of us with a plate of oysters in chipped ice with lemons and horseradish dip on the plates. They put them before us and stood with their white towels on their arms.

The strange part of their suits was that they each had a hole where their shaved cock and balls hung out. The hole was neatly sewn around with black satin ruffles. Their cocks were all rock hard and throbbing in the air.

Briana smiled a wide grin at me. "These are the best oysters in the world, you'll see. These guys have been brought to the edge all day and most recently, the last few minutes, by Prepper. Only after we finish our oysters, are they allowed to come. Their wish is for us to make them come at that time. What do you say Yvette? Are you up for it?"

I looked at the cock before me as he stood there at attention looking over us at the wall. His cock leaked precum and throbbed in the air waiting for release. I pulled on the cuff of his coat. "Do you want me to?"

He looked down at me through the mask. I could see his bright green eyes, eyeliner on them beneath the mask, looking longingly at me. I couldn't make out any other expression due to the mask but I could see his eyes as they opened wide and he spoke deeply and softly. "Lady Yvette, I beg of you please yes, please release me however you wish if I serve you well."

He took an oyster in his hand and with a small fork he scooped it up from the shell releasing it. He pointed with the fork to two sauces. "This one is very hot, this one is mild."

I looked at him again as I spoke. "If I take the hot one in my mouth won't that bother you if I take something else of yours in my mouth?"

His cocked throbbed and he shivered a bit with the thought. "It would feel wonderful!"

"Then I'll save the hot sauce for last, after I've had the oysters. I'll have them plain please." He took the shell and tiny fork and brought them to my lips as he slid the oyster into my mouth. The chilled, salty, fresh flavor of the oyster spoke of its freshness and the taste lit up my taste buds at the back of my tongue. I rolled my eyes with pleasure and looked down the other end at Jenna.

She was painting cocktail sauce on her guys cock with the fork and then licking it off. Briana was sucking her server's cock and she had eaten two oysters so far.

I sipped my champagne and looked at his cock. I put my hand around it and it made my hand look tiny. I stroked him. "Let me know if you get close to coming. I want it in my mouth after the oysters."

He reached down and stopped me from stroking him as his cock pulsed a couple times and a bit of precum leaked. I caught it on my finger and licked it. He presented me the next oyster. I savored that one and another and he stepped back and then filled all three of our champagne flutes.

While he refilled our flutes, I lit a cigarette. I looked at my sheer fingerless glove and the painted nails holding the slender cigarette with a pink stained filter. I recrossed my legs and felt the stockings slide against each other. I felt my one leg rub against Briana's. I bounced that foot which squeezed my cock and made it rub the satin of my dress. Briana took the cock out of her mouth and smiled at me as her server served her another oyster.

I looked back at my gorgeous wife as her hair was draped over her far shoulder and I saw her head bobbing up and down on that cock. It was a gorgeous sight for some reason. She must have felt me watching her as she pulled away from the cock, licked her lips and looked at me smiling. "Nice, isn't it? Are you okay sweetie?"

"Oh yea, just taking a break."

"Now I want us all to finish our appetizers at the same time so when you get to the sixth wait. Here me Briana?"

Briana looked at Jenna and gave her the thumbs up without missing one cock sucking head bob on the shaft in her mouth.

I snuffed the cigarette out in the palm ashtray the server placed before me as he held it in his huge hand. He closed the top of it with a click and put it in his pocket. He prepared another oyster for me as I stroked his cock. He moved my hand away. "Sorry, so close now. Watching you has made me more ready." He held the oyster before my lips and slipped it in my mouth.

He readied the fifth one and served it to me. I tilted my head back and enjoyed the sensation and taste as my earrings dragged across my shoulders. I came back from the pleasure and opened my eyes. I reached inside my purse, took out the lipstick and compact mirror and reapplied my lipstick. I saw his cock jump at the thought of the marks it was going to leave on him.

He prepared the sixth oyster and loaded it with hot sauce. I looked over at Jenna who was also ready for the sixth as she nodded to me. Briana had hers before her lips. Jenna looked at us both and took hers into her mouth. As soon as she swallowed it she dove onto the cock. Briana and I did the same.

I felt the heat on my tongue and lips as his thick velvety cock joined in the heat. A huge come with twelve gushes that I counted rewarded me. His come was slightly bitter and salty. He held back his sounds to a low guttural moan of pleasure with each gush. As soon as he was done he backed away from me, bowed, thanked me and left.

Jenna and Briana's cocks did the same at the same time. Jenna had an orgasm after her server's cock came in her mouth. After he pulled away and left, she continued to hold the little slave's head between her legs while she came. We both watched as Jenna enjoyed the slave girls ministrations. Jenna's body tensed and shuddered for about a minute as we sipped our champagne and watched. All of the male servers passed though the huge doors, which were then shut by the doormen outside of them with a low clunk. Jenna stopped shaking and opened her eyes. She had the slave girl get out from under the table and sent her away.

Jenna lifted her glass. "Not a bad appetizer wouldn't you say girls?"

Briana lifted her glass to her as she rubbed her leg against mine beneath the table. "Perfection Lady Jenna, perfection. Thank you!"

"No thanks necessary Briana. Please, enjoy and help Yvette to enjoy. Yvette? Any remorse?"

I lifted my glass, looked at her smiling widely and shook my head no. I felt my earrings dangle and clink against me. I couldn't possibly have any remorse for that. It was incredible. Of course I had pink pills and blue pills along with alcohol in me and my cock was rock hard. That may have affected my judgment. But right now it felt great. "Perfection!"

The next course was served. In came what appeared to be the same three in the same attire but evidently not, since they were all equally hard and ready as the first three. Their cocks jutted out in front of them as they walked. These servers had main lobster, in the shell but released from it, hand picked and buttered. They moved aside our oyster plates, put the lobster plates before us then cleared the old plates and left to get more.

They each returned with a bottle of fine Riesling, a baked potato, sliced, buttered and sprinkled with parsley, a lemon sliced and wrapped in cheesecloth to hold the seeds in, and candied carrots with a thick maple syrup sauce. They poured the wine into the other wine glasses set for the Riesling, took away the champagne glasses and remaining champagne. Briana's leg danced against mine with her excitement and happiness. "Isn't this incredible?"

I looked into her smiling eyes, as I was sure mine were. "I love Maine lobster, especially one that has had the work done for me. I don't even need to cut the baked potato!"

"Ha ha ha, Yvette, you are something."

Jenna was smiling from her end of the table enjoying watching Briana and I. The servers returned to the room. Jenna spoke to them. "Honorable and beautiful servers, please stand against the walls for us while we eat and keep yourselves ready to come for us when we finish. This you shall do by coming in a glass placed there for it so we can drink it with our coffee. Can you do this?"

They all nodded anxiously. We ate our dinner. The Maine lobster was as sweet as I ever had from the cold-water influence on the meat during the life in the ocean. The butter tasted like fresh Irish butter from cows grazed in sweet green grass and the candied carrots added a crescendo to the sweetness of the lobster. The Riesling chosen was decidedly dry and complimentary to the sweet of the meat and carrots.

I dined immersed in the tastes and sensations of the food barely noticing but being thankful for, Briana's one hand on my knee beneath the table and her leg affectionately, gently, rubbing my stockinged ankle. When we were done and I could fit no more, I sipped the wine and looked at Briana and Jenna as they finished. Looking around the room the three servers were stroking their cocks watching us as we ate. There was something very flattering about that. About them being able to get hard just by watching us eat.

Jenna lifted her hand from the table and motioned to the servers. "Espresso por favor!" The three trotted off with their cocks waging in the air and returned carrying trays with a small silver espresso pot and a small espresso cup on each. They poured our coffees and added sugar or cream as requested by each of us. They all looked to Jenna in their anxiousness.

Jenna took a small crystal glass off the table and held it up to them. Her server took it in hand and the others got theirs from the table by Briana and I. They looked to Jenna and she nodded. Each of them then stroked their cocks a few times, put their heads back and filled the glasses before them grunting quietly. When they were done, they put the glasses before us and bowed, thanked us, turned and left.

Jenna lifted her small crystal glass, toasted each of us as we held ours up to her and we all drank them down. I licked the inside of the glass as it was too good to waste and noticed Briana and Jenna did the same.

Jenna picked up her espresso and came down to us at our end of the table to have it while we smoked. Briana took the cigars out from her purse. "Cigar ladies?"

Jenna took one and sniffed it. "Good idea." Jenna raised her hand and waved at the door. It opened and the girl from the beginning came struggling forward while the doorman held the door for her. Jenna called out to her. "Please, just get us some cigar ashtrays please?"

She stopped her tortured travel, turned and went off. She returned with a tray with three ashtrays and placed them before us. She stood at attention. Jenna responded to her questioning stance before her. "You've done well. Please, relax, have some coffee with us, smoke if you like, and masturbate if you will. Whatever."

The girl's eyes went wide as she stood and began to masturbate, as evidently that was all she wanted was to have some release. Jenna cut the ends off our cigars with her dinner knife and lit each one for us from the silver table lighter. We sipped our espresso and enjoyed the cigars while we watched the gorgeous little sex starved, and highly aroused, woman twitch and shudder before us as she came rolling from one orgasm to the next. She looked at us thankfully as her eyes closed and opened as she progressed through her satisfaction.

Jenna waved to the door once more and it opened. The two doormen stood there. She called them over. "Please, satisfy this woman. Fuck her on the table."

They moved some chairs out of the way down the table from us. They then picked her up like a little rag doll and put her on the table. One of them undid her fetters on her ankles in order to spread her legs. The other one kissed and caressed her nipples. When the fetters were off, the other pushed her on her back, pushed her legs back on the table, and entered her which made her come instantly. They played with her and fucked her as we had our coffees and we watched the show until both men were spent and she had collapsed from being so satisfied. The one that had finished her carried her from the room with her head on his shoulder.

Briana poured herself some more espresso. "Wow, that was incredible. She was so starved for it and so happy when she got it. Isn't that something how it builds like that?"

I certainly knew how that went. Jenna used that on me for some time. Now tonight as well, I was a number of comes behind and the amount of stimulation I had with the cocks and watching all of this and the clothing, well I was horny as hell. "It sure does doesn't it?"

"Well, girls, then I think we should all take in a movie and let our food digest, and then go to the nightclub, drink and dance and have a ball! What do you think?" Jenna slouched down in her chair, rubbed her crotch through her panties and sucked on the cigar as the smoke rolled off of it. She sipped her coffee.

Briana looked at me and held my hand under the table. She raised her eyebrows in question to ask my opinion. I nodded and squeezed her hand. Briana answered her. "We're ready Jenna. A quick stop in the ladies room and we can go to the theater."

That sounded good, a nice, relaxing, engaging, movie with Jenna and Briana next to me sounded like a great way to relax a bit.

A Movie at J.O. Theater and a Corridor of Treats

The three of us went pee in stalls next to each other, touched up our makeup and lipstick together, perfumed ourselves and brushed our hair, used the mouthwash and ended in the waiting area when we had all three finished.

"Yvette" Jenna called to me. "Take three pink pills and another blue one dear." Jenna popped three herself and handed three to Briana along with a blue one, which she took smiling. I opened my purse and took mine. It was a good thing I couldn't overdose on this stuff! "Okay, lets go to the theater. Our entertainment should be ready."

Jenna took Briana by her hand and Briana took mine as we made our way down the carved, wood-walled corridor with thick red velvet carpeting down the center of the marble floors. At the end of the hall was a sign above a double carved door. "J.O. Theater."

Jenna opened the door and entered before us. She led us down the aisle marked at the floor with the dim glow of footlights that shined down from the seats. She stopped after a few feet on the inclined aisle. "As you'll see, the movie is of our dinner. Our fellow theatergoers are presently enjoying it. The Bach that played at dinner could be heard through the sound system. There were three, uh, people? Seated in the center of the theater. I say people questioningly because I didn't know for sure whether they were real or not.

One had a head of a horse, one of a pig and one of a sheep. As we approached, I could make out more detail from the light of the movie screen as it cast its varying glow on the occupants of the seats. Their animal heads all turned toward us as we arrived at their row. The rows were wide open seating rows in which one could walk in front of those seated without difficulty or stepping on feet. They all moved to pull back feet, clad in their high heeled women's shoes, to allow us to enter the seats, even though they didn't need to.

Jenna sat to the left of the one furthest in, the horse head. They were all naked except for the miniskirts made of thin black satin. Their bodies were firm and hard as were the cocks wrapped in the skirts as they stroked them. They turned their heads back to the screen and watched us at dinner as they masturbated.

Briana sat to the left of the pig and I sat to the left of the sheep. I could smell their cologne wafting off of their freshly scrubbed bodies. Briana leaned over the one to her right to whisper to me. I leaned in to her. "Lift their skirts, jerk them off and when they are ready, don't make a mess. Okay?" I could see her evil looking grin in the dim light. I shrugged my shoulders.

Jenna was already jerking off the one next to her and Briana had started with the one by her. I looked at the sheep head and it was looking at me shrugging it shoulders as if to say, "Well?" He took my hand and put it on his cock. I stroked him as he looked at the screen. It didn't take long before he was ready.

Don't make a mess. Hmm. I dipped my head down and put my lips around the tip as he came into my mouth. I swallowed quickly to keep from losing any and he touched my head as he bucked into my mouth.

When he was done, he thanked me with a quick, "Thanks!" and left smoothing his miniskirt down as he walked quickly up the aisle in his high heeled woman's shoes. I could see another guy come from the side at the top of the theater and work his way down the aisle.

I looked back to see Briana and Jenna now with their heads down and their lips on the tips of cocks coming in their mouths as they swallowed frantically and had their heads held as the men pumped into them. The two of them got up and the next one had to wait to enter our aisle. When he could, he sat next to me. A sheep head again. Two more showed up for Briana and Jenna. Another pig and another horse, both in the same skirts and heels with hard cocks ready to go.

I looked at my watch and at the screen showing us having dinner and sucking cocks. After dinner was over, about and hour and ten minutes, I had counted 14 cocks that I made come. With Briana and Jenna we had made 42 cocks come! Counting the ones at dinner, we made six more and then two more got the servant girl. So that's fifty cocks coming in about two hours and twenty minutes.

My cock was hard and ready to come anytime and I tingled all over. Even the palm of my hand tingled from jerking the guys off! I didn't want to mess my dress with come though and I really wanted to come with Briana.

Now I know where the lines of men go. But were we the only ones here for them? Couldn't be. There must be bunches of other women or people like us here doing this. Swingers club? Hmm, maybe this is really a vacation spot for satisfying desires like ours. If so Jenna must have paid a fortune. All these guys couldn't have come cheap with all the great bodies and all. But with the heads and masks, who knows what was under there.

The lights on the screen went dim and the house lights went up a little. Jenna stood and took our hands to have us stand. "This way to the nightclub. We walked down the slanted aisle to the base of the theater and exited through a door into another hallway. This hallway was similar to the last but lit more dimly.

We turned the first corner and the walls had changed from wood to mirrored glass on the top portions and spotlights shined on the wooden carved walls below it. Jenna stood before us blocking the view. "Now girls, this is the hallway leading to the nightclub. It is meant as a work of art, which can be played with and enjoyed. There are two-way mirrors above in which the people above can watch from above. I know we've been very busy tonight but I suggest you partake as it will help set the mood for the nightclub to be able to enjoy and relax better in it. It's your choice what you'd like to do. The artists we will see are here for us." Jenna stood to the side. And we could now see down the corridor.

My jaw dropped. The spotlights each lit a cock that poked through the wall at standing mouth height. It was surreal. Like a bunch of disjointed cocks, each at different states of hardness but each hard, shaved and wet with precum.

I walked closer to look at one. It was real. I turned to Briana. She took my hand and put it on the first one as I was looking down the hall trying to count them all. They faded off in the distance. "Feel it? See it's real. Watch." She jerked it off and licked the tip. It came immediately and she swallowed it up. She went to the next one and did the same, and the next one.

Jenna was going down the other side of the wall doing the same. I started to join them and went from side to side depending on how soon Briana or Jenna finished. We did this for half an hour before we got to the end. I turned around and there were no more cocks in the aisle. My stomach was full of come and I couldn't believe what we had done!

50 cocks earlier and it must have been at least 50 more here since each one came so fast. Divided by three and an average come of one half an ounce at a time, though these all seemed to be more, would be 16 ounces of come apiece! 2 cups, one pint, half a quart almost half a liter! Thank God they've all been tested. I didn't know what to feel but what I did know is I had never been hornier. I was anxious to get to the nightclub but uncertain what lay in store.

Watching, Giving, Getting. Wow!

Jenna exited the hallway into the lobby of the nightclub. The music could be heard from inside. Steven Tyler was belting it out, "Dude looks like a laaaaaady!"

Jenna motioned for us to follow her into the bathroom. When we got inside she stood before the mirror, licked her lips and then spoke to us both. "Girls, now wasn't that awesome! How many girls get to have that kind of entertainment all in one evening? I know it may all seem a bit overwhelming and of course, if we did this every night of vacation it might get old, but think of it as our introduction, our night of excess, our binge. Now the nightclub, I promise, is much less intimidating and of course, as it has been, it's entirely up to us what we do with who when. Personally, I think I'm going to find some strong, handsome men, have them follow me and dolt on me and then have all of them fuck me. For some reason, the number seven comes to mind. Sound good? Everyone up to it?"

Jenna looked at my cock jutting against the fabric. Briana's cock did the same. She yanked the hems off each of our dresses leaving our cocks throbbing in the air. "That's better, let your hair down so to speak girls. Be yourselves, enjoy!" Jenna went into the nightclub as Briana and I looked at each other with our cocks sticking out. Briana made hers grow to the size of mine. I assumed to make me feel more comfortable. She smiled and reached for my hand. I moved my clutch to the other hand and we went into the nightclub. Our dicks bobbed in the air framed by the dress hem, the tops of our stockings and garters.

Jenna wasted no time as she already had one of her studley men, her arm locked into his as they went to the dance floor. Briana looked around and found a nice booth for the two of us to sit in in a quieter, darker corner. She seated herself and pulled me in along side of her until our thighs touched each other. I pulled over an ashtray and lit a cigarette while Briana stroked me.

The waitress came over and smiled as she saw Briana jerking me off. "Hello ladies. Nice to see you're enjoying yourselves. Please don't stop, it's perfectly acceptable here as is anything you might want to do. Can I get you ladies a drink?"

Briana, spoke for us, "Two long island iced teas please."

The waitress spun and took off to fill our order. I had to stop Briana's hand so I wouldn't come. She leaned into me and gave me a kiss on the lips. "I'm so glad you're here. You are so wonderful! I don't know what I'd be doing if it weren't for you." She smiled and pushed my hair back over one ear. I told her thanks and looked over at Jenna who now danced with three guys on the dance floor. She made sure to do dirty dancing with her hands, ass, legs and anything she could use to touch and excite the three guys cocks. Their hard ons all showed under their black pants. Our drinks came and Briana and I sipped them while we watched Jenna. It was only a couple of songs later that she had seven guys dancing with her.

The waitress brought our second drinks and we had just started them when Jenna came over with her train of guys with hard ons and told us what was up. "Hey girls, we're all going upstairs to a more private and comfortable area on the mezzanine upstairs if you'd like to join us!" Jenna flung her long hair over her shoulder, spun and tugged the hand of the first guy and led them to a spiral staircase at the end of the nightclub. Jenna held the long rear hem of her dress up around her knees as she climbed the stairs.

Briana and I followed the group holding our dresses up to climb the stairs as well. When we arrived at the landing we stepped off into a black light lit area with four strange looking chairs side by side in the middle of the room. The only other thing in the room was a kneeler like you'd find in a church pew.

Jenna went straight to one of the chairs and seated herself. She lifted her legs to drape them over padded arms that stuck out so her feet dangled along side of her at the height of her breasts. The guy she was with took her feet in her shoes and lifted them so her legs were fully extended and clamped her ankles into padded restraints that held her feet and legs out from her body at a forty-five degree angle with her toes pointed away in line with her leg.

He then moved her panties so she was exposed and then he pushed four fingers into her as she moaned. She released her breasts from her dress so she could squeeze her nipples. As he was finger fucking her, two of the other guys came over to us and led Briana and I over to the kneeler and gently pushed us down so we both knelt on it. When I turned to the side I could see Jenna now had two other guys by her. One had his cock in her mouth and the other was jerking off watching her.

All the guys were gorgeous and built. They had hard, shaved smooth bodies and huge cocks. It didn't take long for Jenna to take the cock out of her mouth for a second and tell the guy fingering her to fuck her. He took off his pants and shirt and revealed another smooth hard body. I could see his hard cock pop out of his pants and he stepped over in front of Jenna and pushed it in her wet hole while she sucked the other cock and squeezed her nipples.

Her hands then went to squeezing his hard ass and making him fuck her hard and fast. That was when I felt the cock against my lips and I turned to see that all the guys were now stripped naked. Briana was already sucking one cock and the one in font of me slid easily between my greedy lips as I savored yet another velvety tool.

I turned to watch Jenna as my hard cock throbbed in the air in front of me. She was getting pounded in her special chair now and I could tell the first guy was ready to come. He came inside of her and pounded her to an orgasm as he did. As soon as he pulled out, the guy in her mouth, now stripped of his clothes, began fucking her. She held onto his ass the same way and got the pace she wanted from him as the third guy stuck his cock in her mouth.

The guy Briana sucked on then went by Jenna and watched her while he stroked himself and waited his turn. The guy in my mouth moved to Briana and another one came over, took me by the head and once in my mouth fucked my face. I watched as each guy made Jenna come at least once and sometimes as many as four times and then I watched them come inside of her.

When the last two were with Jenna I whispered to Briana, "Please baby, I want you to fuck me in the ass. Please, please, please?" I took Briana by the hand and I seated myself in the chair next to Jenna. Briana helped me with the leg restraints so I was properly exposed to her. She took some lube from her purse and put a few drops on her finger and entered me with that as she kissed me. I looked over at Jenna as she came once more and when she had finished that come she looked at me, smiled and nodded her head.

I could feel Briana now as she pushed the tip of her cock against my entrance. I relaxed the muscle as I had learned to do when putting in my butt plug. She pushed gently and steadily. The pressure made me tingle all over as I felt the hardness beneath the fleshy head pass the now relaxed entrance and proceed down the canal to open and fill me.

The sensation was better than the vibrating plug and actually seemed to have a vibration of it's own. I held Briana's ass in my hands as she started to slowly stroke in and out. The sensation was excruciatingly wonderful as I looked into her gorgeous made up eyes which spoke of the pleasure she was feeling. Briana planted kisses on my lips, face and forehead as she now stroked slowly in and out and made me shudder when she reached bottom. I felt her satin garter belt press against my skin when she bottomed.

Briana whispered in my ear, "Want it bigger?" She pulled her head back and smiled an evil grin as I nodded my head quickly up and down.

I felt her grow inside of me as she did her magic. The pleasure got greater as she did. She seemed to know exactly when to stop and then she resumed her stroking which made me insane with riding the edge of orgasm. Now, when she pulled to almost being out and then pushed herself in till I felt the garter belt, my head rolled back in an automatic response, as if a string was attached it.

My legs tried to wrap themselves around her but they were locked into the bindings, which held them in the best position for my penetration. Briana wrapped her arms around my torso now and squeezed her breasts against mine as she continued to thrust.

I could feel her warm breath in my ear as she began to exert herself. She picked up speed and pushed herself harder and more violently into me. My hands on her ass felt her muscles there hard and silky against my fingers. My body and the chair I was bound to began to shake as she pummeled me. My feet shook in the holders and my body tensed every muscle as the pleasure became overwhelming. My whole self focused on the hard yet smooth and velvety cock that electrified my being.

I looked over and saw Jenna now had her last cock in her and she was coming again as she looked at me. I made Briana pump me harder and faster using my hands on her ass until both Jenna and I came at the same time. I squirted my come all over Briana's garter belt and belly as it shot through the sheer covering. Briana moved back from me, released her hug and put her hands on my throat and choked me slightly as she looked into my eyes with hers wide open and dreamy looking.

Briana then came inside of me. A slight whimper came from her lips as she pounded her come into me with each surge and I continued to come with my whole body even though my semen was spent for now. Briana released my throat and once more wrapped her arms around me and pushed herself and her come deep into me as she kissed me deeply on the lips.

I saw as the last guy removed himself from Jenna and the come of seven men leaked down her slit and dripped on the floor. She lay in her bonds, her legs were still held spread out and raised, and her stocking was torn on one leg. One garter was loose and dangling free of the stocking. Her breasts were red from the squeezing and they still sat high above the v-neck of her dress, exposed and gorgeous. Jenna's nipples were still hard, shiny and wet from being sucked. Her long black hair was messed around her face.

Jenna rolled her head to the side, her eyes half open and smiled at Briana and I. She spoke quietly with tiredness in her voice. "That felt so fucking good! I have to do that again. How was your virgin fuck Yvette? I saw Briana pounding you pretty good. Was it the best thing you ever felt or what?"

I nodded, closed my eyes and put my hand in Briana's hair. I kissed her neck and smelled her sweet perfume while Briana gently stroked her semi hard cock inside of me. I felt someone undo my ankles and legs and I wrapped them around Briana squeezing her to me. I think we fell asleep and someone carried us to bed since that's where I found myself next.

Cages, Milking and Truth

I felt the sunlight on my cheek as I rolled over and felt Briana along side of me. We were both dressed in short silky nighties. Briana felt me against her and pulled me under her. She pushed her cock against mine as she scrubbed us together while she thrusted her hips slowly. My hand automatically went to her ass as I rubbed against her and felt her hardness and it's desire.

Briana whispered in my ear, "Oh God! You make me so hot!" I reached down and wrapped my long nailed hand around both of our cocks holding them against each other. We both pumped our cocks against each other that way. The feeling was dreamy having that smooth velvety cock of Briana's against mine. She had made herself the same size as me and we both fit neatly in my hand as we stroked together.

I felt Briana crush me to her as all her weight fell on me as she came in my hand and I came at the same time. We shuddered against one another as the semen fell wet and sticky on my belly. I released our cocks and Briana pushed against me in the wetness sliding against my cock with hers. We fell asleep again.

We both woke up at the same time and we showered together. We washed each other and enjoyed ourselves once more. I found a pair of jeans and a tee shirt and put them on and walked barefoot to breakfast with Briana dressed in a sundress and heels. Jenna was seated at the table working on her laptop as we took seats her table.

A warm breeze blew across the patio and brought the familiar smell of the pines once more. Grapefruits were brought to us with poached eggs, fresh blueberry muffins, fresh squeezed orange juice and coffee.

I bit into the muffin as Jenna looked at me with an inquiring tilted head. "What's with the jeans and tee-shirt? No makeup? Look at Briana and look at you. Why the slob? You practically look like a boy!"

I swallowed the sweet treat, drank some orange juice and looked at Jenna while she waited for my reply. "I, uh, I don't want to do what we've been doing. I feel like a slut and want to stop taking those pink and blue pills."

"Why dear? You think those pink and blue pills are making you like that?"

"Well, of course they are!"

Jenna reached into her purse and took out two small boxes of candy. She dumped them both out on the table. "There, those are your pink and blue pills. Candy, nothing more. It was yourself being given the freedom to be yourself that made you the way you were. Not the pills. The pills just allowed your psyche to free itself from constraint. What you did, and loved doing, was because it's in your nature to do so."

I played with the pills, read the boxes, crunched them instead of swallowing them and tasted the sugar. "Really? These are them?"

"Really." Jenna looked at me sternly. I averted my eyes from her feeling ashamed.

"I see your shame. Nothing to be ashamed of! You're not normal whatever normal means. Never have been. This is what you are. You're not a real man."

"I am a real man!" Jenna looked at me laughingly while she stood and pulled her panties down and kicked them off her foot. She came over to me and undid my jeans while I sat. She pulled them down to my ankles. She slipped my panties under my globes. My ever hard dick stood at it's comically small attention. Jenna straddled me and slipped my cock into her. She squeezed me inside. "Okay, fuck me and make me come." I looked at her while she rode me up and down in little lifts of her bottom while her legs straddled the chair. I came shaking as I did.

Jenna got off me. "Real man? Come on Yvette!" She went to her purse and took out my metal cage, which she put my now wet cock and balls into and she locked the lock. There my cock sat, no longer being able to get a full erection. No longer able to come until she was willing to release me from it. "Now, if you think you're a whore and being a bad girl, then be a good girl. Let's see how long before you beg me to take this off."

There I was, sitting on the patio in front of everyone after my wife showed what a man I'm not. I pulled my panties back over the cage and pulled my pants up. I walked away.

What was I to do? I hated the thought that I really was, by nature, a whore. Not just a whore but a freak whore that was a genetic male that loved dressing up in women's clothing and, to make things worse, has a cock for a brain that wants nothing more than to satisfy men, watch my own wife fuck and please other men, (and imagine it's me being fucked when she is) and enjoy the sensualness of life. I was a freak that wanted to make as many men come as I could and always wanted really nothing more than to do all of that. That can't possibly be the real me! If it were, how would we ever be able to pay for vacations like this that would have to happen almost every day? I had to be my old self, a wimpy guy that wrote awesome software.

I didn't believe her that the pills were fake. It had to be them that did that to me. I resolved to enjoy the rest of our week just lounging around, reading, and not taking any pills.

It went okay that day. At dinner I had to watch as Briana and Jenna once more feasted as we had last night. Jenna insisted that I accompany them to the movies, hall visit and nightclub as well. There I stood in my jeans and tee shirt as I watched them once more cause somewhere around one hundred ejaculations. Watching them both enjoying themselves and watching all those guys come was sheer torture.

I told myself that it was just a carry over from having been taking all those pills and once they were out of my system it would stop.

It didn't, my cock continued to strain against the cage the next day as well. It was then that Briana tried to bring me some relief. It was just before dinner after her and Jenna had both gotten dressed. "Sweetie, it must be killing you not coming for so long. I think you might feel better if I helped a little."

"Do you have a key?"

"No, but there is a technique that will release some of your semen though you won't really have a full come. At least it might make you feel less crazy. Take a shower and clean yourself out down there and I'll show you."

I showered and came out in a plain terry cloth robe, already familiar with what Briana was to do from the times before when Jenna used it on me. "Okay baby, kneel down here on the bed and put your bottom in the air."

I climbed up on the satin topper and Briana put a plate under my cock. She had me lay my head on my arms on the pillow. I felt her put a cold vibrating object in me. "You'll see, this will be pleasant but not great. It's called milking. All I have to do is get this on the right spot and you'll be milked out."

Briana maneuvered the object around until she felt satisfied that she had found the right spot and then she turned up the vibrations while pressing it against that spot inside of me. That familiar on the edge of coming feeling was there now and I immediately started to ooze come onto the plate through my caged yet eager cock. It felt like coming but without the throbbing and pulsing and of course, without being fully hard. It did feel very nice. She kept at it for only about thirty minutes nuzzling me and caressing my body while she worked it inside of me and I oozed continuously. I could have done it all day.

"Mmm, thanks Briana, that felt wonderful."

"No thanks necessary sweetie. I feel so bad for you. Why don't you just get over your feelings and be what you are honey? I miss you being a part of it."

"I can't."

"Suit yourself. You should be able to tell the pills had nothing to do with it. I can see how you want to join us. Stop fighting yourself and just accept yourself for what you are."

Briana picked up her purse and took Jenna's arm as they walked out for the drink before dinner. I followed them once more and watched and longed for it. My libido was not much satiated by the milking I received.

I lasted until Saturday night, which was to be our last night there. When Prepper came into the room this time I let her prep me. I was once more a beautiful woman with a cute cock. Prepper couldn't undo my lock though. Only Jenna could.

Jenna came into the dressing room and stood there. She looked at me in my white satin, bubble hem, mini dress with white stockings, garter belt and six inch white strappy heels. Prepper had done my hair beautifully, accenting the texture in the shag. She had chosen white and gold earrings that dangled to my shoulder and clinked together as I walked. My breasts were once again full with nice cleavage though now, I really, really wanted them to be real.

"Yvette! You look wonderful. It's so good to see you get out of those jeans! Does this mean you've come to a decision? Can I take off the cage?"

I nodded at Jenna, somewhat embarrassed to admit that I was ready and anxious to play. It was the last night we'd have at this vacation resort and I didn't want to miss it.

"I'm so sorry Jenna that I missed all the other nights. I wish we could stay longer but I can imagine what this all must have cost us. And, uh, do you have any more pills?"

"Oh sweetie. Now that you have decided, we have to take that cage off first!" Jenna came over, took the key from her purse and she released me. I immediately got hard feeling the cool air against it as well as the dress, which slid silkily against it.

Jenna stood and gave me a big hug. She spoke excitedly now with her excitement showing in her animated movements as she walked around looking at me and adjusting my clothing, accessories and hair just right. "I love you so much sweetie and I'm so happy for you that you now can be what you are and that you actually want to."

"Do you want the breast implants, cheek, butt and hip implants and electrolysis? We can still do it and be back here in a couple of weeks being all ready to go at it with your new body!" Jenna smiled broadly and looked at me as she held me back with her arms. She looked into my eyes and gauged my response, her intelligence saw that I was totally converted now. I couldn't keep the smile from my face and eyes. "Wonderful! See, I was serious about the pink and blue pills really being candy pills! Nothing in them. You haven't had any for days now. It was your own self that made you that way since that is what's inside of you."

"Oh my God! So I got so, uh, so good feeling just by thinking they were real? I just gave myself permission basically and the feelings and sensations were because that's the way I am when I release my paradigms and give myself permission? I guess your right."

"Of course I was right. That's why even though you haven't had any for days you still wanted to dress and play tonight. It's a part of you."

"But Jenna, how can we afford all of this! It must cost a ton to pay for all these guys to serve us!"

"Oh, by the way, the butlers and so on are almost all part time volunteers since they enjoy the free sex. The others dear, they uh…" Jenna hesitated and walked away from me then swept a circle around and came back standing before me. She looked at me intently now making sure I got the message she was delivering. "The man named Roster keeps track of what is going on for proper billing."

"God! How much does it cost to pump a quart of come out of guys in one night? I couldn't imagine what it would cost us."

"Honey, it's not how much it costs! Wasn't it a wonderful feeling being able to make them all crazy and like putty in our hands? Well, hard putty for a while in our hands…and of course, wherever else we put them."

"Well, yes, but at what cost?"

"Again honey, it's not what it costs uh, it's actually how much it uh, makes for us. You alone made six thousand dollars the first day! Briana and I have made over forty thousand dollars this week! Ha ha ha. I already turned in our resignations and put our house up for sale. I knew you would come to a good decision. This is our place, our, uh, men's club. I bought this as an investment some time ago wondering what to turn it into. We'll live here. Now we can get paid for what we really enjoy doing and I will ALWAYS be satiated completely at the end of the night as will you. By the way, taking it in the bottom is your highest paying trick so you might want to think about how much you enjoy that and offer it to more men." Jenna came over and kissed me gently on the cheek so as not to leave any lipstick or mess my makeup.

"So we're whores? Oh my God!"

"No dear, not whores, professional administrators of pleasure! YOU, are no longer a virgin call girl like when you arrived. You are an experienced professional and certainly not virgin! So lets get to work! If that's what you can really call it when it feels so good! Life is good, do what you want and enjoy what you do." Jenna grabbed my arm in hers and we flew out of the room to where Briana was walking down the hall to meet us. Briana took my other arm.

"Welcome to the team lover! How about dinner, with some luscious appetizers, a movie, a short stroll down a long hallway for desert and some nightclubbing!"

I walked in powerful minced steps in time with Jenna and Brianna as we all clicked on the marble floors in our six-inch heels. I felt my body tingle all over and my cock swished against the underside of my dress as my fake boobs bounced. I couldn't wait to have real ones and all the other changes now! I can come as much as I want to now, always, everyday and I can really make others feel good at the same time too. Bottom trick is the highest paying huh? Hmm. I am what I am. A professional administrator of pleasure. Life is good!

V.C.G.

V.C.G.

1

Made in the USA
Monee, IL
08 March 2024

54684219R00095